Diana didn't wait for an answer. She turned on her heel and marched up the sanctuary aisle.

Scott caught her at the door and turned her to face him. "There is only one lie in my profile," he said.

"Which one?" she asked.

"This one." He pulled her into his arms and delivered a kiss that curled her toes. Diana thought that phrase was the stuff of books or movies. It wasn't a real condition. People's toes didn't curl. But hers did. Her arms went around him. This wasn't like the kiss at the wedding rehearsal. There they'd had an audience, and even though she hadn't remembered they were present, Scott had. Here there was no one. They were together and alone. His mouth took hers in the sight of stained glass windows, vaulted ceilings and the polished wood of the entry hall. Diana didn't think of where they were. She didn't think at all. She felt. She let his mouth tease hers and sweep deeply into a recess of pleasure that had her groaning with delight.

SHIRLEY HAILSTOCK

began her writing life as a lover of reading. She likes nothing better than to find a quiet corner where she can get lost in a book, explore new worlds and visit places she never expected to see. As an author, she can not only visit those places, but she can be the heroine of her own stories. The author of over thirty novels and novellas, including her electronic editions, Shirley has received numerous awards, including the Waldenbooks Bestselling Romance Award and *Romantic Times* Career Achievement Award. Shirley's books have appeared on BlackBoard, *Essence* and *Library Journal* bestseller lists. She is a past president of Romance Writers of America.

His LOVE MATCH

SHIRLEY HAILSTOCK

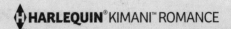

HARLEQUIN® KIMANI™ ROMANCE

To my sister Marilyn for all the joys and memories we made and for all her acts of kindness.

Recycling programs for this product may not exist in your area.

ISBN-13: 978-0-373-86342-6

HIS LOVE MATCH

Copyright © 2014 by Shirley Hailstock

HARLEQUIN®
™ www.Harlequin.com

Printed in U.S.A.

Dear Reader,

When you hear the word *bride,* don't happy emotions and images of a white gown with a long train come to mind? Your wedding is the happiest day of your life, and the planning of that event is worth all the trials you go through to get to it. In *His Love Match,* our heroine Diana gets to experience that happy feeling every time she helps a bride make the memories of a lifetime.

However, for Diana, those memories are on hold until an old college friend enters her life in the most unusual way. I hope you enjoy a good wedding.

Happy endings,

Shirley Hailstock

I'd like to thank Hilda of the Hildarling Bridal Shop. Hilda was kind enough to give me a job in her shop when I was thinking of buying the establishment. While I never went into that business, it was great fun and proved a valuable experience for this and my other novels regarding brides, grooms, weddings and the accoutrements of marriage.

Chapter 1

It can't be him.

Diana *knew* him. No computer would do this to her. Not twice in one day. Diana Greer sat at the table of the local coffee shop across from Princeton University. Her usual unshakable demeanor had just taken a hit. The place was geared up for the lunch crowd, and both students and white-shirted lawyer types poured in like Christmas shoppers just before closing on December twenty-fourth. Glancing through the wall of people, her gaze darted around bodies, hoping against hope that what she looked for wouldn't be there. Her heart sank when the human sea cleared for a second and confirmation forced a groan from her throat. He had the DVD in his hand. The one they had agreed to both carry as identification. The cover photo faced her, despite his hand cutting a wedge out of the romantic couple. There was no mistake. It could be a coincidence, but Diana doubted it. It was her suggestion that they identify themselves using this method. She'd seen it in more than one movie. Usually it was a rose or a book. She hadn't thought the suggestion would prove so close to the Hollywood version of a couple who met online actually knowing each other. She could kick herself for not insisting on a photograph before they met. But not knowing what he looked like had been intriguing, romantic even. And they were only meeting for lunch. Opinions on vanity could be judged then.

She had to get out of the shop before he saw her.

Glancing at the ceiling she cursed the universe for its wretched sense of humor. "This is not funny," she muttered. People at a nearby table looked to see who she was talking to. She smiled quickly and dropped her head, choosing to stare at the golden liquid in her cup. Maybe there was some way she could get out without him seeing her. Diana looked from side to side. She was hemmed in. The tables were very close together and crowded with patrons. She knew it would be rude to leave without talking to the man she'd spent three months corresponding with through email. But if anyone deserved being stood up it was Scott Thomas.

He looked around, stretching his neck although he already stood head and shoulders above everyone else in the place. He was obviously looking for someone—her. Diana looked down as he almost made eye contact with her. Instinctively she knew it was too late. He'd seen her. And her copy of *You've Got Mail* lay square and center on the table in front of the chair she saved for him—one she'd stopped three people from taking. She wished she had something to hide the DVD with, a book or scarf— even a napkin would help. But she had none of those things handy and Scott was already weaving his way through the crowd toward her.

"Diana?" He frowned, coming to stand in front of her. "Is that you?" He deliberately slipped his DVD into his suit pocket. "What are you doing here? I thought you were meeting someone for lunch?"

Of course, he knew she was meeting someone. Hadn't

she told him so this very morning? Diana raised her chin and looked him in the eye. It can't be him, she told herself again, as if the thought could transform this man who'd stood in her office only an hour ago into someone else—anyone else. *Just, please, God,* she prayed. *Not him.*

In her office that morning their encounter had been less than friendly. She wasn't in the mood for another one. Scott had come to the office to persuade her to move out and find other accommodations for the business she'd run there for the past five years. Their encounter had been unfriendly, and Diana was reminded of the sarcasm he'd subjected her to while they both attended the university that was only a few steps from where they stood now. Nothing appeared to have changed in the intervening years. He was still on the opposite side of everything she did, said or wanted.

And for no reason. At least none she could discern.

"I was just leaving," she said. As she moved to stand, he picked up the DVD. Diana flopped back down as her knees refused to hold her in position. At once Scott glanced from the DVD to her, then back again. Diana watched as he pulled his own copy from his pocket and realization dawned in his dark brown eyes.

"There has to be a mistake," she said, reaching for her copy. Scott glanced at both covers.

"I believe there is."

Diana grabbed for her DVD but encountered resistance from Scott. As she raised her eyes to him, she saw that playful disapproval that had been there when they were college students. Quickly it disappeared and he released his hold on the case.

Getting up, Diana inched around the crowded table and started for the door. It seemed as if the universe was mocking her. A line of people that hadn't been there before now stood between her and the door. She would need to wait to get out of the place, when all she wanted was to get as far away from Scott as possible. Around him she couldn't breathe. It had always been like that. Even all those years ago, when they were in college and he would harass her whenever he could, she found it difficult to breathe in his presence. Apparently time had not changed that reaction, either.

There was another door, she thought as she looked over her shoulder. She'd try to get to it. However, when Diana tried to turn around, she realized it was a mistake. Scott was directly behind her, and her body was now in contact with his. Despite the air-conditioning, her temperature flew off the scale. She was surprised she didn't double over in pain from the bends. And it didn't help that Scott's arms instinctively came up to steady her. The urge to lean into him was so great that she grabbed his hands and pushed them away with more force than she intended.

"I apologize," she said. "I'm under a little stress." That was more than the truth. Stress followed her, sat on her shoulder, worked its way into the marrow of her bones any time Scott Thomas's name came up or even entered her mind. And having him close enough that she could smell his cologne and feel the heat of his body threw her back to the one other time in her life when she was this close to him. Close enough to kiss. That time there had been a kiss. He'd kissed her. Devastated her. Left her wanting more when the passion that flared within her burned deep and hot and out of control. When it ended as abruptly as it had begun, he turned and ran away. She watched him disappear. Then she fled, too. Running across the campus in the opposite direction from the one he'd taken, competing with the wind for dominance.

And that had been the last time she'd seen him until ten months ago when, practically on the heels of his attorney's exit, he'd walked into her office and doubled the offer if she would vacate her offices. She refused.

She hadn't told her online friend about the encounter. She needed to keep Scott Thomas relegated to a corner of her brain that was as inaccessible as possible. Lately the folds in that area were vibrating with the need to access the data stored there.

"I guess leaving through the rear door is out of the question," Diana said, her voice slightly breathy.

Scott glanced over his shoulder. Looking back at her, he said, "It's just as crowded over there."

Diana turned back. She held her breath, relieved that he was no longer touching her, but still aware that he was close enough for her to feel the heat of his body. How could MatchforLove.com have paired her with Scott? They had nothing in common. Nothing except she owned a wedding planning business in a complex that he wanted.

Diana was not moving.

Finally the crowd at the door moved and she was on the street. Taking a full breath, she felt as if she could gulp the air. Not looking back, she started up Nassau Street intent on reaching her car and getting as far away from Scott Thomas as she could.

A hand curling around her arm stopped her. Diana turned, taking two steps backward to keep some distance between them.

"At least we can be civil," he said.

"If this is another of your attempts to get me to give up my offices, it's not going to work. As I told you this morning—"

"It has nothing to do with the property," Scott interrupted her.

Diana shifted her weight but said nothing. If he didn't

want to make another pitch to get her offices, what did they have to discuss?

"How do you think we ended up here together?"

"Obviously by some computer glitch."

Diana knew it was a mistake to follow her partner Teddy's urging. Diana had told her that she didn't have time for a man in her life, but Teddy, in her usual persistent manner, had worn her down, and finally Diana had gone into the MatchforLove.com system and filled out the profile. And now she stood in front of Scott Thomas, a mistake if she ever saw one.

Before he could continue their conversation, his cell phone rang and Diana took the opportunity to leave. She felt she'd get to her car and be done with him. At least when she turned the corner at the end of the block she could relax. But Scott was not to be eluded. He fell into step next to her, all the while continuing his phone call.

"What?" Diana heard him say. He stopped walking, but caught up with her several steps later. "Can't you find someone else?"

He listened for a moment while she walked faster. Her shoes were the latest style, very high heels on a small platform. They elevated her five-foot-five-inch height by five additional inches.

"All right," he said as if giving in to something.

Diana got to the corner and turned. The garage was half a block away. Hoping Scott would continue up Nassau Street, her thoughts were doused as he turned with her.

"Yes, I said I'd do it." A moment later he nearly shouted into the receiver. "What did you say?"

Diana couldn't help listening while she walked.

"Who's doing it?" he asked.

Again there was a pause.

"You're kidding!" Scott said. This time he sounded as if something incredible had happened.

Diana didn't get the impression that there was any kidding going on. But she heard Scott agree to the final unheard question. "It's all right. I get it. I'll be there." He ended the call and pocketed the phone.

Diana could tell something was not as he wished it to be, but she wasn't interested in finding out what was off in his world. She had her own to deal with.

"Why are you following me, Scott? I have a high-profile wedding to get the final plans on, and I don't have time to be bothered with childish pranks. You've already said it's not about the offices, so what do you want?"

Scott hesitated a moment. "I want to know if you told the truth."

She frowned, not understanding his question.

"On your profile. Was everything you put in there true?"

Anger, hot, red and eruptive sliced through her like the knife edge of an arctic wind. "As I remember it, lying is *your* department. And since we aren't likely to see each other *again*..." She emphasized *again,* closing the door on him making further offers on her offices. "I think we should just forget this day ever happened."

Pivoting on shoes that were now hurting her toes, Diana straightened her back and shoulders and walked away from him. He didn't follow her, a good choice on his part, she thought. Practically calling her a liar to her face was enough. Another word from either of them would require police protection.

"How was he?" Theresa "Teddy" Granville jumped up from her chair the moment Diana came through the office door. "Was he as good-looking as we thought?"

Diana dropped her purse on the chair and gave Teddy

the look. It should have been patented between them. It was the look they gave each other when a bride chose something that was totally wrong for her theme.

"That bad?" Teddy was nonplussed. She flopped back down in her chair. "After we had such high hopes."

"After *you* had high hopes." It was at Teddy's insistence that Diana go to MatchforLove.com. Diana had done it to silence her partner. But after she began talking to F9021@MatchforLove.com, things changed. He seemed to understand her. Even though they never identified themselves by name, he knew she owned her own business and she knew he flew airplanes. She thought he was a pilot.

"What was wrong with him?"

"He was Scott Thomas."

Teddy came forward in her chair as if she'd been pushed. "Scott Thomas? The Scott Thomas who wants us to move? *That* Scott Thomas?"

"One and the same," Diana said.

"That's impossible."

"I couldn't believe it myself. It was all I could do to get out of the coffee shop."

"Without seeing him?"

"Unfortunately, no," Diana said. She took a seat in front of Teddy's desk. The place was neat as a pin, although Teddy was juggling three weddings for the next two weeks. It was time for the brides to get crazy and the mothers of the brides to go ballistic over something minor. Luckily at this moment the phones weren't ringing with complaints. "I wished I could have become invisible when I saw him, but he spotted me and we talked."

"Talked?"

"We both agreed that the dating service had made a terrible mistake. No way are we compatible."

"That's all?"

"Pretty much."

"Pretty much, what?" As usual Teddy read between the lines and persisted.

"As we were parting he called me a liar."

"What?" Her eyes grew big.

"Not in those exact words. He asked me if everything I put in my profile was true."

"Well it was, wasn't it?" Teddy asked.

"Teddy!"

"I mean," she stammered. "We all like to embellish ourselves a little online."

"I did not *embellish*."

At that moment the phone rang. Diana got up to leave. At the door Teddy stopped her. "Well, at least he's good-looking," she said.

Diana frowned at her and went to her own office. It was a contrast to the orderliness of Teddy's. Diana worked in chaos. She knew where everything was, and she could put her hands on it without error.

Good-looking, Teddy had said. Diana supposed if she thought about him without the animosity that clouded his image, Scott was pleasant to look at. More than that. He had great eyes. They were probably his best feature, dark brown, fringed by long lashes. His cheeks had dimples that drove the women crazy in college. They hadn't diminished in effect in the ten years since they graduated. He wasn't a football player, but his lean features boded well for the diving team. Diana remembered the broad shoulders that tapered to a thin waist and strong muscular legs. Diana had to admit he *was* good-looking. If she was planning one of her bridal fashion shows, he'd be a shoo-in for a tuxedo model.

Diana glanced down at her desk. Several bridal magazines lay open in front of her. One by one she scanned the pages and studied the grooms. Not one of the men smiling up at her had an ounce of the gorgeous good looks that Scott Thomas had.

Looks weren't everything, she thought. The man was still a jerk. And even though he could turn the head of every woman in town, Diana knew the two of them should never have been matched.

Scott loosened his tie and opened his collar in the same instant he came through the garage door into the mudroom. As usual the house was cool and quiet. In the kitchen he opened the refrigerator and grabbed the container of orange juice. It was nearly empty. He lifted the container to drink, but his mother's words came back to him, and he poured a glassfull and drank it in one long gulp.

The answering machine showed eight new messages. Aside from his sister, people usually called or sent text messages to his cell phone. It was unusual for anyone to contact him on his landline. Checking his cell, he found another nine unread texts. As he scrolled through them he felt both grateful and disappointed that none were from Diana. Why he should expect to see anything from her, he didn't understand. She'd made it plain that there could never be anything between them, so why would he think she'd call? Apology, maybe. He shook his head. That was unlikely.

Pressing the button on the answering machine he listened to the calls. Most of them were either from Bill Quincy or his bride-to-be, Jennifer Embry, a couple who'd talked him into being a member of their wedding this afternoon while he was on the street with Diana. Bill thanked him for standing in for Oscar Peterson, who'd been in an accident and would be laid up for the next several weeks.

He'd recover, but not in time for the nuptials. Jennifer, a numerologist, wouldn't have her numbers thrown out of whack. Scott knew she'd postpone the wedding before doing that.

The other calls were from Jennifer giving him details of where and when he needed to be. She called to change his tuxedo appointment twice.

The reason he agreed to stand in for Oscar was that Bill had told him the wedding was being planned by Diana's firm. At the time he thought it was ironic and he wanted to get him off the phone. But now he was sorry he'd agreed. Impulsiveness wasn't one of his traits. As a pilot he had to be steady and thoughtful, but Bill was a friend. To stand up for him, he'd make the sacrifice. Scott felt no disappointment at not being included in the original plans. He could do without weddings. Being involved in one was something to be avoided, like air pockets and bumper-to-bumper traffic. He was sure when Bill called him, he was last on the list and the only one available.

Scott was committed now. He had an appointment for a tuxedo fitting, and his name had been added to the programs. Jennifer expected him at the rehearsal and the rehearsal dinner. The wedding was the following weekend.

The answering machine clicked off. Scott grabbed the television remote and pressed the power button. He smiled to himself. What was Diana going to think when he showed up at the wedding rehearsal? He remembered her strutting out of sight as she walked into the garage. Her parting words told him that she never wanted to see him again. She was wrong. She'd see him. And sooner than she thought.

He'd angered her. There had been times in the past when he'd intentionally intimidated her, but today that wasn't his plan. They had rubbed each other the wrong way since their first meeting. While he'd followed her to the garage, she could have heard only one side of the conversation he was having—*if* she was listening. He was sure she was. In his experience, women always listened. But Diana had never followed the mold. He couldn't say he knew her, but he knew that beneath the facade of calm she showed to the world was a smoldering woman. He'd found that out when he kissed her on campus in broad daylight, a lifetime ago.

To think that all these years later, he could still remember that kiss. *Her* kiss. Scott had kissed his share of women. They seemed to hover around him like skydivers in formation, but none of them were memorable. None but Diana.

And next weekend he'd have another chance to piss her off.

Scott didn't know how long he'd been waiting, but he was getting irritated. He had a flight today, and he needed to get this fitting done and return to this office. Pulling out his phone, he reviewed his missed calls. His sister Piper's number and her photo appeared on the display. He couldn't help smiling. The photo was taken at her wedding four years ago. It was of the two of them, their faces near replicas of their parents. He should have returned her previous call, but with all the appointments this wedding required, it slipped his mind. He pushed the send button and waited for her to answer.

"Hi," she said. "I've been dying to talk to you. How was the meeting? What did she look like? I have a thousand questions. Did the two of you connect?"

Scott laughed from deep in his belly. His sister was a nonstop talking machine. He sobered and tried to decide how to begin and how much to tell. He should have thought of this before he dialed her number. He'd tell her about the meeting. He could describe Diana, give Piper all the answers she wanted, but he would leave out the fact that the woman in question was Brainiac.

"Well, go on. Tell me," she commanded. "Is she the woman of your dreams?"

"I'm not sure about that."

"Did she meet all those ridiculous requirements you put in?"

"I haven't found that out yet," Scott said. "We only met for lunch. I didn't have time to interrogate her." Scott's forced laugh took the sting out of his words.

He went through describing Diana. He told Piper she had dark hair, omitting that it was lustrous and fell over her shoulders and down her back like a cascading waterfall. He shared that her eyes were brown, but he didn't add that they were like looking into melting pools of coal. He said she was dressed in business clothes, but didn't say that the suit hugged her curves the way his hands wanted to or that her shoes supported legs that were as long as the Garden State Parkway.

"Did the two of you connect?" she asked.

"In a way," Scott hedged, knowing his sister would not let that go.

"What do you mean?"

"Remember the woman I told you about when I was in college? The one with the long hair."

"You mean the one who always had her head in a book?" Piper asked. "Didn't you call her something? Brain something. Yeah, Brainiac."

"Her name is Diana Greer." It was her, but Scott didn't want to tell his sister. He'd said so many things about Diana that were not flattering that he didn't want Piper to have a more negative picture of her than had already been painted.

"Was it *her?*"

"It was her," he admitted.

Piper laughed for a moment. "It's like that movie. You probably don't know it. It's a chick flick—*You've Got Mail*. The couple don't realize they know each other. It has–"

"I know the movie," Scott interrupted.

Piper seemed to sober. "I'm sorry this didn't work out, Scott." Piper was the only person he'd told about the matchmaking service. Of course she supported him. She always did. "I remember you said she had so much hair that when she had her nose in a book, she looked like Cousin Itt."

Scott winced at that. "She's changed a lot."

"I hope so. " Piper paused. "Are you going to try again?"

"This is not over yet," Scott told her.

"You're seeing her again?" Surprise was evident in her voice.

"At a wedding next weekend." He forced a laugh for the second time. "I'm a replacement in Bill Quincy's wedding. Diana's company is the wedding consultant."

"From what you told me, I thought she'd be running General Motors by now. She's a wedding consultant?"

"Actually she owns her own business. Weddings by Diana. She's got stores in several states. While they might not be General Motors, if you put her up against the president of GM she could hold her own."

"Oh." Piper held on to the word as if it was the end of a song. She sounded impressed.

"You've heard of them?"

"Who hasn't? She's been all over the financial pages. It seems everything she touches turned to green, that's as in money. Her franchises have been expanding like they were a fast food chain. I wish I'd used her when I got married."

Scott felt his heart tug at that. When he saw Diana he was impressed that she had changed over the years, but her changes were for the better. He supposed she was always there under the hair and out of the book, but he rarely saw her or even looked at her. It wasn't until that one day in front of Nassau Hall that he saw her face. It was naked of any makeup. Her skin was flawless, and the depths of her dark eyes were enough to drive a man crazy.

And where she was concerned, he was all male.

Chapter 2

The parking lot of Darlington Wedding Gowns and Tuxedos was packed when Diana pulled into the only available space. And that was as far from the door as she could get. Darlington had been several steps away from her offices, but with Scott's new use for the property practically everyone had relocated. The store was now housed in a huge strip mall several miles from her.

Final fittings for the Embry-Quincy wedding party was scheduled for today. Diana wouldn't let anything having to do with Scott deter her. She stepped into the June heat and felt her clothes and body deflate. It shouldn't be in the nineties this early in the season. And she shouldn't be here. First she was the owner. She worked with the managers of new locations and Teddy ran the consultant staff. But Jennifer Embry came from old money, and she insisted Diana consult her wedding. As such she was the wedding planner, not the dress approver. However, she'd learned early in this business that a wedding planner's duties were fluid. Some brides were demanding. Others only wanted her to take care of the ceremony and the reception. But she and Teddy ran a soup-to-nuts organization.

Pulling open the door of Darlington's, she silently

thanked the air-conditioning gods for their invention of such a useful mechanism.

"Diana," Jennifer greeted her with a relieved smile. "I'm glad to see you."

Jennifer stood in front of a triple wall of mirrors, her white gown billowing around her.

"You look beautiful," she told her client.

"The hem is too long. The gloves aren't the same color as the gown. I can't see through the veil."

Susan Dollard, the store owner, frowned. Diana smiled back at her.

"Jennifer, remember we know that items of different materials will not be exactly the same color due to shine, weaving methods, difference in lots, and a hundred other reasons. Just focus on the day. It's going to be beautiful. I know the alterations will be completed while we wait."

The seamstress was on the floor with her needle and thread, quickly adjusting the length. Diana stepped back to get a good look at the bride. "You look gorgeous. Just wait until Bill sees you in this gown."

The praise wasn't false. Jennifer glowed in her gown. It was a perfect fit and style for the tall, majestic-looking blonde.

"The veil, Ms. Embry." Susan came forward with the altered crown.

"Let me," Diana said, reaching for the soft concoction of netting. Stepping up on the platform with Jennifer, she placed it on her head and spread out the folds of fabric. "Is it better?" she asked.

Jennifer turned back to the wall of mirrors. Tears were in her voice when she answered.

"Great," Diana said, glad to have appeased another bride. She stepped off the platform and onto the floor. "How's everything else?"

"Fine," Jennifer said. Then she turned to Susan and the seamstress and apologized. Both women smiled. They'd been through this scene a hundred or more times. "Oh, by the way," Jennifer said. "There's been a replacement for one of the groomsmen."

"I got your message." She should have said *messages*. Diana wondered if three was a significant number for Jennifer. She'd told her three times about Oscar's replacement, yet she never mentioned who the replacement was. Brides, even those as organized as Jennifer, had lapses of memory.

"He's next door getting fitted for his tux."

"Let me go introduce myself." Diana liked knowing the members of the wedding party. In case of an emergency, she knew who she was looking for. She took the digital camera she always carried from her purse. She'd take a photo and label it to be sure. Jennifer Embry had twelve bridesmaids and an equal number of groomsmen. It was impossible to keep all the names straight, even though Diana was good with names and faces. Still, she relied on file photos to help her or one of her assistants in case she had to delegate duties.

The gown and tuxedo shops were connected by a short passageway. It was designed both to keep the noise down and to provide privacy. Diana didn't use it. She preferred to enter from the outside.

The bells chimed when she entered the shop. Several people browsed the various colors and styles of men's clothing. All of the dressing room doors were closed. Judging by the parking lot, the place was full.

"Jeremy," she called.

The clerk came from the last dressing room. "Ms. Greer, how are you?" When they were alone Jeremy was very informal and called her Diana; occasionally and with several drinks under his belt, she was Di. When she came in the shop, she was Ms. Greer. To her he was always Jeremy. He and Susan were man and wife, but they kept to their separate areas unless need forced one to the other side of the causeway.

"I'm looking for the new member of the Embry-Quincy wedding. The bride told me he was here and I wanted to introduce myself."

Someone said something from behind them and one of the other clerks went to aid the customer.

"He's waiting for his fitting." Jeremy indicated one of the dressing room doors.

"I can wait a few minutes."

"It might be longer than that. I'm short-handed and swamped. Three parties are due in any moment now and I have all the dressing rooms filled." Suddenly, he put a hand to his chin. Then he looked at Diana with a strange expression. "I wouldn't like to impose, but you do know the ropes? Do you have a moment to help out?"

Diana never refused Jeremy anything. He'd helped her get started by giving her mountains of advice that saved her from some major pitfalls. Before his move to this location she had worked in his store for over a year and had learned how to take measurements.

"The Embry-Quincy wedding is in the Red Room." He smiled and offered her the tape measure hanging around his neck. "I believe the new member may need his nerves soothed."

Diana smiled. She'd often been called upon to settle a guy whose mind was on other tasks. She glanced at the dressing rooms. Jeremy named his rooms after those in the White House. It gave the place a little elegance, he said, and who wants to dress in Room 3 when they could have the Red Room? Diana still remembered the expression on

his face when he gave more credence to a false name than
to a nondescript number.

Taking the tape measure, she dropped her purse in his
office and knocked lightly on the door of the dressing
room. "I'm here to take your measurements," she said before going in. She wanted the man to know she was female in case Jeremy had told him to remove his pants. Or
if he was shy.

"Come in."

Diana stepped through the door and quickly closed it.
Although Jeremy's dressing rooms were huge and set up
like the entrance to a home, with a foyer section and a comfortable living room, sporting a large mirror that covered
one wall, Diana couldn't be sure the client wasn't standing
near the door in full view of whomever was outside. When
she turned back she saw only her reflection across the spa-
cious gray-colored carpeting. The subdued floor contrasted
with the bright furnishings. Walking several steps past a
wall that set off the foyer area, she came face-to-face with
the last person on the planet she expected to see.

Diana didn't know which one of them was more surprised.

"What are you doing here?" they asked at the same time.

Diana recovered first. "I'm here to take your measurements if you are the replacement in the Embry-Quincy
wedding."

"Scott Thomas, nice to meet you." He extended a hand
as if they'd never met. Diana ignored it and he folded
both arms across his chest. The action brought his white
shirt up a little higher over legs that were long, strong and
naked. She wished her heart didn't step up its beat, but she
couldn't deny it. Teddy had put the thought in her head
that he was handsome. That was an understatement. He

was a crowd standout. And with him half dressed, Diana wondered what he'd look like totally naked.

Clearing her throat and mentally shaking those thoughts from her mind, she asked, "Shall we get started?"

"I didn't know you worked here."

"I agreed to help Jeremy out because he has a lot going on in the shop. And I expect you have other places to be."

"As a matter of fact, I do."

"Then…" She pulled the measuring tape from her neck and took a step forward. "That is, unless you'd like a male to take your measurements. They're all busy right now, so your wait will be a little longer."

"I've waited long enough," he said. "Let's get it over with."

Diana took a deep breath and approached him. "Turn around."

He presented his back to her, and she reached up to measure its width. Then the length of his arms. She tried doing his waist from behind, but he turned in her arms. Diana caught her breath. For a moment she didn't think she'd be able to keep her feet on the floor. Gripping the tape measure, she fought to keep control of her shaking hands. Finally, she dropped to the floor to measure his inseam.

"Spread your legs, please," she said. Blood hammered in her head. She could feel the heat of his nearness. Her face flamed as blood rushed up her features, burning her ears.

"Why don't I just tell you my size?" Scott asked.

For a short moment Diana was unsure what he meant. Then sanity returned, and she realized he meant his suit size. She could feel more heat pump into her face and ears, and she wondered why they didn't melt and slide off. She dared not look up at him.

"Your suit size is not always the same. And you want

to look your best at the wedding." Diana couldn't imagine him looking any other way.

"Of course. Anything less and Jennifer will have my head."

Diana raised herself up on her knees and prepared for the final measurement. She willed her hands to remain steady. Swallowing and ignoring the roar of blood and unwanted memories inside her head she touched his leg just above the knee. It was a test of her own ability to continue this procedure. She'd done this hundreds of times. She'd measured guys who were model perfect, silver-screen-idol caliber, and never had to keep her emotions in check. But Scott Thomas was throwing her usual calm into aggregated chaos.

His leg was warm, as strong and solid as a tennis player's. She moved the tape measure higher. Time seemed to slow down, and her hand moved with the slowness of passing years on its way to the juncture between his legs. The catch in his throat and the heat of his body found a place in her brain that told her to get the measurements done as quickly as possible. But that instruction didn't reach her hands. She pulled the tape measure down and extended it to his ankle, then to his sock-clad feet. Unconsciously, she brushed against him. His arousal was hard and he jerked away from her touch.

Diana's head snapped up and she met his eyes. They were dark, almost liquid. She'd seen that look directed at her only one other time. And from the same face that now stared into hers with a longing so deep it wrenched her heart.

Scott reached down and pulled her up to him. She stood as if reaching for the sky. Scott's body was long. Diana climbed the mountain of him until she was on her feet. She could feel the full length of him. For a moment she luxuriated in the warmth that covered them like a shared aura. They faced each other, their mouths only a kiss away. *Kiss.* The word registered in her brain. Lightning speed brought her up short. She pulled free of Scott's arms and hurried to the door. With her hand on the knob, she turned back.

"I apologize," she said. "I'm finished with you. You can dress and leave."

Outside, Diana stood breathing hard, clutching the tape measure as if it was an anchor keeping her pinned to the ground. She took several breaths. What had happened to her? What was she doing? She'd never done anything like that before, but this time she found it hard to control herself. She wanted to touch him, wanted to keep running her hands over his hair-roughened skin. She wanted to feel his arousal, allowing him to lengthen and grow in her palm.

Stop! she screamed at herself. She had to calm her thoughts before Jeremy emerged from one of the dressing rooms. He knew her well enough to tell if something was happening to her, and there was no doubt in her mind that something *had* happened. And more would have happened if she'd let it go on any longer. How could she feel this way? She hated Scott Thomas. She'd always hated him. How could she want to kiss her? Oh, God, how could she want to have sex with him?

She gasped at the thought. Was that what that was? Had it been so long since she had sex that she wanted to have it with a man she didn't even like? Diana stopped all thoughts of Scott. He was probably dressed by now and would open the door behind her at any moment. She didn't want to be standing there when that happened.

Rallying her thoughts, she took the card with Scott's information to Jeremy's desk and gave it to him.

"Thanks for the help," Jeremy said. "I think everything is in control now." He surveyed the shop.

Diana smiled quickly, wanting to get out of the shop before Jeremy saw how close to falling apart she was. And worse, having to face Scott so soon after she'd had her hands on him and her body melded to his. Gathering her purse, she air-kissed Jeremy and left by the connecting door, escaping into the bridal shop and out of Scott's sight. Diana didn't think she exhaled until she had finished with Jennifer's needs and returned to her car, all without seeing Scott a second time.

But there would be other times. Now that she knew he was the replacement groomsman, the two would meet at the rehearsal and the wedding. Thankfully, she did not have to attend any wedding activities with him. When the rehearsal and wedding ceremony were done, so would she be. Then she could return to her normal life. Whatever normal was. Or had been. Would it be the same ever again? Diana didn't really think so. She and Scott both lived in Princeton. The township was small even though the borough covered a larger space. They both lived in the township, and according to the card she'd recorded his information on, he lived within a good walk of her residence. Diana's business was there. She'd called it home for years not realizing she could run into Scott at any point in the day.

And for the next few days, it was inevitable.

The National Cathedral in Washington, D.C., might be larger than this one, Scott thought, but only by an inch or two. Scott should have known Jennifer would plan something this elaborate. Bill was a lot more laid-back. Or was it Diana, the wedding planner, who'd suggested this mammoth structure? Scott scanned the height of the ceiling, then brought his gaze back to the door. Where was Diana? Most of the wedding party had arrived, but Diana had yet to appear. She'd been on his mind for the last three days. Since the incident in the dressing room she'd plagued him day and night. He'd thought of her all the time. Questions arose for which he had no answers, and every question led to another. He wanted to know where it would lead, *if* it would lead anywhere. He wasn't even sure he wanted it to lead somewhere.

A few days ago he'd been a relatively happy man. Now a woman was driving him crazy. He wasn't even sure she knew it.

And there she was.

Diana opened the cathedral door and slipped inside. She walked fast down the aisle, and she looked as if she'd been running. She wore jeans and a bright pink short-sleeved sweater that accentuated her breasts. Scott remembered her pressed against him. Immediately his body began to harden. He stepped aside, forcing himself to relax.

"Sorry," she said to Jennifer when she reached her. "The flight was late and traffic delayed me."

"We're still on schedule," Jennifer said, taking a look at her watch.

"Well, let's get started." Diana put her jacket and purse on one of the pews along with a large bouquet of flowers. When she turned around, her eyes met his. Quickly she looked away, giving her attention to the rest of the party.

"Father Ryan is here," Jennifer stated. The priest came through the back of the church. He wasn't dressed in robes but wore all black, pants and shirt, no collar.

"Ladies, gentlemen, could we line up in the back of the church."

"Where's Bill?" Scott asked. "Shouldn't the groom be here?"

"He won't make the rehearsal," Jennifer explained. "His

trial went to the jury yesterday. They're waiting for the verdict."

Scott thought she should be prepared for these events to interrupt other occasions in their future, but he kept his words silent.

"He'll meet us later at dinner."

Diana took over then, putting people in order by height. She explained what the church would look like in the morning after the flowers and candles were delivered and lit. She cautioned the party to be careful with the candles with their headpieces, since the netting burned easily. Couples were paired together. As the music played, they practiced their walks down the aisle.

"It's time for the bride and groom," Father Ryan said.

"The groom isn't here," Jennifer told him. "He won't make the rehearsal."

"We'll need one of the groomsmen to stand in for him." Father Ryan looked over the small assembly.

The guys looked from one to the other. "Several of us are already married," one of them said. "We've done this before. Scott, you need the practice. Why don't you stand in for Bill?"

"I'll do it," Scott agreed. He knew if he didn't it would start a back and forth banter about the state of his bachelorhood. He's been on the end of that conversation more than once and had no intention of allowing it to happen in front of a dozen women, most of whom did not know the circumstances that had led to the needling.

Scott remembered a time when they were all single and had no intention of marrying. Then one by one, they fell off the wagon. He was the last unmarried soul on that wagon, and while the guys often complained about their wives, they loved them and wouldn't trade their new lives to return to the old ones. Of course, now that they were in their thirties, their days of drinking and bar hopping all night had morphed into attending nursery school plays and walks in the playground. Occasionally they'd get together for the male bonding ritual in front of a big-screen television as their favorite teams vied for dominance on a Sunday afternoon, but at night they returned to the woman they loved.

Scott's transformation had been to the sky. Although he'd learn to fly as a child, accompanying his father on trips, Scott had made a career of flying. While piloting wasn't a sport, pilots were like athletes. They aged out early and needed a second career. He'd decided on his, but one woman stood in his way. And that woman stood at the back of the cathedral.

"Stand over here," Father Ryan said, indicating a space inside the gated nave. "The best man should stand next to you."

One of the groomsmen separated himself and followed Scott.

"Clark?" Diana called. "Remember to let Bill know the two of you will enter from that door in the back. She pointed to the door on the right side of the nave. "Father Ryan will lead you out."

Clark nodded and the two men assumed their positions.

"Now, the bride." Diana turned to the bridesmaids, who were fanned out in front of the bar separating the nave and sanctuary. "Who'll stand in for the bride? She can't do it. Bad luck, so the story goes."

As the woman looked from one to the other, they each refused to step forward.

"Ladies, there is no legend related to standing in for the bride."

"Diana, you can do it?" Jennifer said. She checked the time, and Scott understood she was keeping everyone on schedule. Not only was Jennifer a numbers fanatic, but watches could be set by her plans.

"I can't," Diana protested.

Scott stared directly at her. She wasn't looking at him, but he wondered if his agreement to stand in for Bill had anything to do with her not wanting to be Jennifer's surrogate.

"Someone do it," Jennifer ordered. "We don't want an overcooked dinner." Jennifer lifted the bouquet of flowers Diana came in with and stared at the group. Slowly they each shook their head. Eventually, she came to Diana.

"All right," she said, taking the flowers and her place at the end of the aisle.

As Diana headed down, Father Ryan gestured for the two men to come forward and take their places. Scott had a clear view of Diana as she started down the aisle. She came toward him. She was beautiful. Gone were the baggy jeans and unkempt hair that, aided by a book, hiding her face from view during their college days. She wore designer clothes, trendy shoes. If Scott hadn't seen her a few months ago when he'd come to negotiate her office lease, he'd have sworn the two women weren't one and the same.

She floated down the aisle. Scott's eyes saw the church as it would be, bathed under the yellow glow of candlelight, a white lace gown and Diana as the bride coming toward him.

Him! he shook himself. He wasn't marrying Diana and she wasn't the bride. This was make-believe, and his imagination was working on Stress Level One if his thoughts continued along their present course. He looked at her again, checking to see if her eyes were on him and if by some telepathic relay she'd heard his thoughts.

She wasn't looking at him, but she was smiling. Her staccato steps keeping time to the rhythm of the "Wed-

ding March." Jennifer smiled at her from the front pew.
The groomsmen looked at her with appraisal in their eyes.
Scott stepped forward as she came to the bar. He wanted
to take her arm and pull her close to his side. The groom
wouldn't do that tomorrow. He stood close to her, blocking any view the other groomsmen might have.

"I won't go through the vows," Father Ryan said. "At
this point tomorrow, I'll be the first to congratulate the
bride and groom." He glanced at Jennifer. "Then you will
kiss and turn to go up the aisle." He paused a moment,
confirming the procedure with Scott before remembering to look at Jennifer. "Okay?"

Jennifer nodded.

"Not quite," Scott replied. All eyes focused on him. He
took the flowers from Diana and handed them to Jennifer. Then facing Diana he put his hands on her waist and
pulled her toward him. She didn't know what he planned
to do until his mouth was on hers. She went rigid for a
moment then she relaxed. Her mouth tasted good, chasing
away his logical thought processes. She opened her mouth
and his tongue swept forward. He felt her hands take his
elbows. The fabric of her sweater brushed against his fin-
gertips, a movement as erogenous as his wet mouth sweep-
ing over hers. Her hands began a slow climb, but stopped
when someone behind them cleared her throat. It was like
a spark to his brain. Logic returned and Scott pushed at
her arms. Quickly he ended contact. "Now, we turn and
walk up the aisle." He didn't recognize his voice. Then
taking her hand, he started toward the rear of the church.

Diana dropped his hand when they were out of earshot
of anyone else. "Don't you ever do that again," she hissed.

Like a quick-change artist, she walked back to the congregation. All heads and all eyes were on her, but the silence in the cavernous cathedral was like a tomb.

"Father Ryan, is there any other instruction?" Diana asked, her voice strained. It gave Scott a joyous feeling to know that she had been affected by what had happened between them. His action wasn't impulsive and he enjoyed having Diana in his arms, but to provide such a public display was not his style.

"Only, good luck tomorrow," Father Ryan said.

Everyone smiled and seemed to relax. Diana could hear their sighs.

"Then I'll say good-night." Diana turned to Jennifer and gave her a wide smile. She didn't know if Jennifer was trying to put her at ease after Scott's kiss, but she was grateful for the apparent relaxation in the atmosphere. "I'll see you tomorrow morning."

Jennifer smiled and Diana moved up the aisle.

"Jennifer, Diana has to go to dinner with us," Scott said. "It'll throw the numbers off if she doesn't go."

"Oh no," Diana protested. "I've just returned from Montana. I'm tired and I need to get some rest. Tomorrow is an important day. And Bill will be at the restaurant. The numbers will work."

"Not a problem," Jennifer agreed. "See you in the morning."

Diana moved to leave. Scott stood in the middle of the aisle. "If you've just returned from a plane ride, you must be hungry. Surely you can eat before you leave."

It was no secret to anyone in the church that Scott wanted her to go with him. He didn't care what they thought. The groomsmen smiled and gave him their silent approval. The bridesmaids only looked stunned.

"I'll get something at home," Diana told them. Her voice hadn't returned to its normal level yet.

She pushed past him and continued up the long aisle. Scott watched her go. But he wasn't finished with her. He'd wondered about her for two days. Why would the computer choose her for him?

He needed to find out. He was going to find out.

Chapter 3

Diana shut her refrigerator door with a sigh. There was nothing to eat in there that didn't require thawing and at least an hour of cooking time. She was hungry now.

She would have gone to dinner with the party if Scott hadn't thrown her off balance with that kiss. What was he thinking? And in front of people she worked for! She wasn't a member of the wedding. She was an employee—granted, a controlling and directing person, but she was still being paid for her services. He'd flustered her so that she forgot she hadn't bought food because of the trip to Montana, and she didn't think to stop and pick something up before pulling into her driveway.

She was in no mood to go out now. She'd make a peanut butter and jelly sandwich and wish she had some milk to go with it. Then a warm bath and bed would round out a long day. Tomorrow promised to be just as long and stressful, but once the reception was underway, Diana would be free to leave. And hopefully put Scott Thomas out of her mind and out of her life.

As soon as she got the peanut butter from the cabinet, the doorbell rang. Frowning, Diana wondered who would be dropping by without calling. Padding barefoot to the door, she checked the side windows and jumped back. Her heart skipped a beat or two, then hammered in her chest. Scott was out there. What was he doing there?

"I saw you," he said through the door. "Open up."

Diana hesitated a moment then taking a long sustaining breath she unlocked the door. "What do you want?" she asked, blocking his entrance.

Scott held up a pizza box and a bottle of wine. "Since you couldn't come to dinner, I brought it to you."

"How do you know I didn't already eat?"

"I assumed." He raised his eyebrows. "And it is an assumption that because you've been out of town, you didn't buy food before you left."

"I could have stopped somewhere before I got here."

"But you didn't." His voice was teasing. "Are you going to invite me in? I'll let you share my dinner."

Diana hesitated a moment. She smelled the cheese and tomato sauce. Her stomach growled. "Didn't you go to the rehearsal dinner?"

"I did."

"Then you can leave the pizza and return to the bachelor party. I'll get your money for the delivery," she said, reducing him to a mere driver. "I'm sure you'll have much more fun with your friends."

Her comment didn't seem to touch him in any way. He stared at her with the same boyish grin he had when they were students and he was chiding her for some infraction of his personal rules.

"Can't. They had shrimp in the salad. I'm allergic to seafood."

"You know everyone in the wedding party. I'm sure they'll miss you."

"Let's see." Scott tucked the wine under his arm and leaned against the doorjamb, holding the pizza box in two hands. "Sit around with a bunch of guys and drink while watching X-rated movies versus sitting around with a beautiful woman while drinking and…"

"There is no *and*," she finished for him, even though him thinking she was beautiful made her heart do something close to a tribal dance. "The party's at the Marriott. I'm sure you can find it." Diana pushed the door to close it, but Scott proved both agile and quick. Taking the tiny space she used to step back, he slipped past her and into the room.

"Nice house," he said, looking around. He walked through the foyer and into the main living room. With just a few steps he'd taken ownership of the place. He moved as if he had a right to be here. "Is this the way to the kitchen?"

Diana closed the door and said nothing. She hadn't been in Princeton that long, but when she chose this house, it was because the kitchen was state-of-the-art. While the business kept her out of it most of the time, Diana loved to cook.

Scott walked to the great room-kitchen combination. Diana found him making himself at home as he looked through cabinets for plates. Her shoes lay in front of the sofa and the television was muted on an old black-and-white movie. Even though she was taller than the average woman, Scott dwarfed her, especially since she was without her five-inch shoes.

"Where do you keep the wineglasses?" he asked, still moving comfortably from cabinet to cabinet.

Diana went to the china cabinet and took out one glass. Coming back, she set it on the dark granite countertop.

"Aren't you having any?"

"You're assuming the glass is for you."

"You wouldn't throw a guy out on a cold winter's night

without a glass of his own wine." Although his voice was completely sincere, he was still teasing, and Diana wasn't in a teasing mood.

"I wouldn't," Diana told him. "But it's June, not January. And while it is night, I need a clear head tomorrow. I've had a long day and a plane ride, wine is not a good choice for me."

"Where did you go again?"

"Montana."

"Montana," Scott echoed.

"My partner, Teddy, usually takes care of the wedding planning. I do some of it when we're busy, but mainly my focus is on additional franchise sales and operations."

"Is Teddy a man or a woman?"

It wasn't the question Diana expected. She wondered why he wanted to know. Most people wanted to know about franchising: what it cost, how was set it up. Or how she got into building her own business. "*Her* name is Theresa Granville."

Scott nodded. "So, Weddings by Diana can be found in how many places?"

"Right now we're in six states. I'm working on adding Montana." She left it at that, not going into detail about the difficulties she was having. She was sure they would iron out soon and things would return to normal.

Scott placed two slices of pizza on each plate and offered her one. "Are you putting me out or eating with me?"

Diana's stomach growled in answer.

The kitchen was too intimate. It was huge, a chef's delight with light blue walls and rich cherry cabinetry. The appliances were stainless steel, and everything was coordinated. Diana could easily see her sister and brothers gathering here for a meal, talking over old times and catching up on their lives since they were last together. But she couldn't sit here with Scott. The space would be too personal, too open to confession. And she didn't want him to learn anything more about her than she was willing to expose.

Taking her plate, she went to the great room and wedged herself in the corner of the long sofa. Stretching her legs in front of her, she rested the plate on her lap, preventing him from sitting close to her. He took a place on the love seat across from her.

Diana took a bite of the pizza triangle. "What is Jennifer going to think about you throwing her numbers off?"

"I don't know. She'll probably force the waitress to sit down just to keep the table balanced." They both laughed. Diana relaxed a moment. Scott could be charming and funny when he wanted to be. She had only seen a couple of sides of him, the angry landlord and prankster college student.

"Why did you come here tonight?" she asked. Diana didn't know if he'd tell her the truth, but she wasn't a person Scott ever sought out. He was perfectly content to let her remain a face in the crowd unless he wanted to embarrass her in some way.

"I brought you dinner."

Diana acknowledged it by glancing at the plate and the box he'd carried from the kitchen and set on the square coffee table between them.

"I see, but you were out with a lot of people who know you well enough to include you in their wedding. Yet you left them to come here." She paused. "You said it had nothing to do with my offices. So what is the draw?"

"You sell yourself short," he said.

Diana laughed. "One thing I don't do is lie to myself.

We never got on all those years ago. We didn't get along when you tried to evict me."

"I never tried to evict you," he protested.

Diana went on as if he hadn't spoken. "And at the coffee shop we agreed the computer should never have matched us. So, I don't understand why you're sitting in my great room eating pizza and drinking wine, when you could be letting go at a bachelor party."

Scott set his wineglass on the table. His plate, now holding only crumbs of cheese and a slosh of tomato sauce, was set next to it. He leaned back in the chair and stared directly at Diana. She didn't think he was going to answer her. Finally he stood up. Diana thought he might go to the door and leave. Her heartbeat increased. She wanted him to both go and stay.

He did neither. He moved around the coffee table and stood in front of her. Diana bit her bottom lip to keep it from trembling.

"I came by because when we stood at the altar tonight you kissed me."

"I kissed him." Diana was dressed for the wedding, which was scheduled to begin two hours from now. She liked to be at the bride's home an hour before she was to leave for her last ride as a single woman. Often there was chaos, and dealing with that needed a level head. Unsure if that would be the case today, Diana hunted for everything she needed. The trip to Montana and her return yesterday hadn't given her time to come to the office and make sure she had everything. Consequently, she'd risen early and dropped by before going to Jennifer's.

"You did what?" Joy spread across Teddy's face like the sun rising. "Where?"

"In the church." Diana searched for her scissors. Finding them, she hooked them on the inside of her jacket. The outside was lace, but the lining held a myriad of possible necessities. Diana wanted to be prepared. Nothing could go wrong today.

"Why?"

"He volunteered to stand in for the groom, who wasn't there. And the bridesmaids were too superstitious to stand in for Jennifer. You know Jennifer's many beliefs. Apparently her friends are just as bad. So I ended up doing it."

"But you're not supposed to practice the kiss," Teddy said, her eyes following Diana as she moved from place to place collecting supplies.

"I know that. It was Scott who started it."

"And you finished it?" Teddy questioned.

"Not exactly." Diana stopped searching and turned to look at her partner. She wanted to tell someone. She wanted to explain her feelings and have someone sympathize with her. Teddy was the perfect choice, but Diana was unsure of her feelings. She hadn't had time to process the changes that she saw in Scott or the way she felt about him. And there was still the matter of her offices. Could he be using this tactic to get her to do what he wanted?

But the worst part, the reason she couldn't explain everything to Teddy was she didn't even realize kissing Scott was anything but natural. They stood at the altar. The ceremony was over. Father Ryan said, *Kiss the bride,* and Scott kissed her. She'd fallen into his arms so easily, it was as if she belonged there, that it was natural for her to be there. She'd become unaware of the other people in the church until she'd heard Jennifer clear her throat. She would have remained in his arms and gone on kissing him. Thank goodness Jennifer interrupted them.

"Did you like it?" Teddy's voice intruded on her thoughts bringing her back to the office.

"It's been a long time since anyone kissed me."

"I'll take that as a yes," Teddy said.

"Well, I only have to deal with him for one more day." Diana went back to getting everything she needed. "Once the ceremony is over and the requisite photos are taken at the reception, I'll be out the door faster than she can get the white off that dress."

Teddy laughed. It was a saying they used to mean the consummation of the vows. Diana's mother had coined the phrase and the two women adopted it.

"How did you get out of the church without explaining?"

"I asked Father Ryan if he had any further details to share. Then I left."

"Your face must have been burning."

Her entire body was burning. Even now, she felt the heat of last night. "I think that's everything," Diana said, finally feeling she was ready to leave. She looked at her desk, her bag of essentials, her notebook, assessing that everything was in order.

"What are you going to do about it?" Teddy asked.

Finally Diana looked at her partner. "About what?"

"About your attraction to our landlord. Maybe you can use that attraction to get him to back off about the offices."

"Teddy!" Diana was appalled at the suggestion. "Have you stopped to think that his attraction for me, if there is an attraction, may be for the same reason?"

Teddy's happy face turned to one of concern. "I hadn't thought of that."

"Think about it." Diana looked around one more time, then checked her watch. "I have to go. You've got everything under control here, right?"

She nodded. "My wedding isn't until five, so I'll head over to the bride's house this afternoon."

"See you tomorrow, when we can go back to business as usual." Diana threw the words over her shoulder as she headed through the door.

"Wink at him during the reception…maybe ask him to dance," Teddy shouted at Diana's back.

Diana wouldn't even make eye contact with him if she could help it. She wanted things to go back to the way they were just twenty-four hours ago. She'd been on a plane from Montana. Anything after she arrived at the church she wanted expunged from the universe.

That would include his kiss, a voice spoke in her head. Diana stumbled and twisted the toe of her shoe on the broken parking lot pavement. A large gash appeared in the front.

"Damn," she cursed. "This is Scott's fault."

Everything was his fault. Well most of it. From the moment she walked on campus ten years ago until he left her house last night, he'd been a thorn in her side. After the wedding today, she didn't want to see him again. He could deal with her lawyer regarding their offices if any more discussion was necessary—and as far as she was concerned, there wasn't.

So life could go back to normal. Diana thought it, but she didn't feel it. She knew something more would happen, something unexpected. Scott wasn't the type of man to just drop things. He had a plan in mind, and Diana wondered what it was. She needed to be on guard for whatever he might spring on her. His appearing at her home last night was unexpected and designed to throw her world out of kilter.

He'd succeeded.

Diana took a deep breath as she parked along the curved driveway of the house where Jennifer lived. The street and drive leading to the house was ringed with cars. Only

Jennifer would have a procession leading to the church. For days workmen had been setting up for the reception. Thankfully, the weather was cooperating.

Getting out of the car, Diana went to the trunk and changed her broken shoe for another pair. She had learned the necessity of being prepared for every contingency. Not only did she have extra shoes, she had several changes of clothes in case they might be needed. Diana turned and took a long look at the cathedral. She'd done a few weddings here before, but this was the first one where she felt as if a huge weight was on her shoulders. Even when she first started and bluffed her way through her first solo as a wedding consultant, she hadn't been this nervous.

The limousine arrived carrying the bride. Behind her car was a succession of stretch limos carrying the twelve bridesmaids. Diana greeted the bridesmaids and ushered them into the rooms set up for them. Then she accompanied the bride. Jennifer truly looked wonderful. Her face had that bridal glow to it. Or was it that she was so in love with Bill that it was visible? For a moment Diana envied her. She wondered if she'd ever look like that when she thought of a man.

Jennifer had a perfect day for her ceremony. Diana assumed all the numbers had clicked into place, and from this point on Jennifer's life would be on the schedule she'd set up for herself.

Diana could only hope her own life had a plan. She thought it did. Or it had. Until a few weeks ago when an innocent cup of coffee had thrown her world into chaos. Maybe she should have given up the offices and been done with any dealing with Scott. But fate wasn't on her side. Fate had brought him to this wedding. Even if she had agreed to relocate, he would still be an honored guest at the head table. But they wouldn't have stood before the altar. He wouldn't have come to her apartment. And she wouldn't continue to feel the tingle of his mouth on hers.

"We're ready," Diana told the bridesmaids as she shook thoughts of Scott out of her mind. A hush settled over the women as if everyone was afraid of opening night. "Just do what we rehearsed. It'll all be fine."

She looked at one particular bridesmaid, younger than the rest. Her color was paste-white. "Breathe," Diana said. "And smile." She gave the girl a smile, and after a second the girl returned it. Diana leaned close to her and whispered, "Even if you fall on your face, it won't be a catastrophe. One of those hunky groomsmen will rush to your rescue." The girl tried to hide her laugh behind her hand. Diana pulled it away and watched as she relaxed.

One by one the bridesmaids floated down the aisle. Diana stood up from her crouching position as the ring bearer and flower girls took tentative steps down the long aisle. As Jennifer embraced her father's arm and headed toward wedded bliss, Diana breathed a sigh of relief. It was almost over for her. So far she'd avoided making eye contact with Scott, although she'd felt his eyes on her several times. She knew he was looking at her by the heat that surged through her body and inched up her neck. Everyone else would think it was exertion and stress from making sure every detail was going as planned. Scott would know differently.

"You may kiss the bride," Diana heard the priest say. She couldn't help remembering Scott's kiss on her mouth. The church organ started to play, and the bride and groom rushed down the aisle as man and wife. Scott looked directly at her as he went by. Diana kept her eyes on Bill and Jennifer.

As the bridal motorcade—that was the only name she could think to call it—arrived at the reception hall,

Diana wanted to run and hide, but she couldn't. She was in charge. From the second car, Scott was the first person to step out. He turned to help his female companion, and Diana ushered them toward the reception line. The assembly moved like a coordinated dance. Jennifer and Bill led the procession and took their assigned places in the reception line. Obligated to go in, Scott moved away from Diana, a bridesmaid on his arm. As he passed he whispered, "You can't avoid me forever."

Diana didn't say anything. Not that she had time. He was already three couples ahead of her. She followed the last of the party. Her duties didn't take her into the reception hall, but she looked in to make sure every detail was as Jennifer had requested. Scott was shaking hands with the guests, but when she looked at him, his eyes found hers as surely as if they were destined to connect. Diana wanted to look away, knew she should, but she didn't. She withstood his stare, trying to prove that she wasn't avoiding him. The war of their eyes only lasted a few seconds before Scott had to give his attention to the next guest in line. To Diana it felt like it lasted an eon.

"You've done a wonderful job," Jennifer's mother whispered when the reception line broke up and the group headed for the dais and the sit-down meal. "Jennifer looks so happy."

"She does," Diana agreed honestly, passing a tissue to Mrs. Embry.

"The flowers, the dresses, the hall." Mrs. Embry dabbed her teary eyes and shook her head as if it was difficult to take it all in. "The church was just lovely."

Diana handed the woman a second tissue.

"Thank you," she said. "I never would have believed Jennifer could look so beautiful."

"She's a beautiful woman," Diana said.

"I know." Her mother patted her hand. "But today…
today…"

"She glows," Diana finished for her. Taking Mrs. Embry's arm, she led her to the head table. Scott, who was
already seated, got up and met them. "Would you help her
to her seat?" Diana asked.

Mrs. Embry was not an old woman. She was overcome
with emotion. Jennifer was her only daughter and today
she gave her away. Their lives would never be the same.

"Mrs. Embry," Diana called. "It's not goodbye. Your
lives will be different and better. In a year or so there may
be grandchildren."

Mrs. Embry looked at her for a long time. Then she
hugged Diana. "You're a treasure," she said. "You'll be
just as beautiful a bride someday as Jennifer is today."

The compliment should have made her feel good, but
the fact that Scott heard it made Diana cringe inwardly.
She thanked Mrs. Embry and took a step back. Scott accompanied her to her seat. Diana turned and headed for
the bride and groom, who were standing at the end of the
dais and waiting for everyone to be seated so they could
have the full attention of the room.

"Jennifer, Bill," she said with a smile. "It was beautiful. I hope you liked it."

"Everything about it," Jennifer said, her smile wide and
happy. "Thank you so much."

"I just wanted to say congratulations again, and since
my duties are over, I'm heading home for a relaxing day.
Tomorrow, I start again."

"You're not leaving?" Diana didn't have to turn around
to know Scott's voice. Ignoring him, she addressed the
bride and groom. "Enjoy your honeymoon and have a wonderful life."

Jennifer leaned forward and hugged her. Bill kissed

her on the cheek, and the couple moved away to visit their other guests.

"I wore this tuxedo just for you. Look how well it fits."

Diana was reminded of the episode in the dressing room. Her face flamed. She could feel the heat rising and her ears burned as hot as the sun.

"Good night, Scott." Pivoting, she headed for the exit and her SUV.

"You know if you leave, I'll just come by your house tonight," he said.

"I don't have to answer the door."

"I'll make a racket and wake up your neighbors."

Diana stopped walking and turned to face him. "You live in Princeton, right?"

He nodded.

"Then you know how responsive the police force is. I'll call them and tell them you're being a public nuisance."

"I'll tell them you're only acting like this because I kissed you."

Diana felt a lightning bolt jolt her. "What is it you want?" she asked. "We already know we're not compatible. The computer made a mistake. Why can't we just go our separate ways. Unless…unless this constant meeting has another purpose."

"You wound me," Scott said, placing a hand over his heart. "Seriously, the office has nothing to do with this."

"Then what does?"

"I'm intrigued," he said.

"You said that before—and believe me, I don't take it as a compliment."

"It is. I think we should talk. We could start with a dance."

Diana glanced at the empty bandstand. "The band won't begin until after the meal. The combo will play soft music to accompany the food, but the dancing begins in another ballroom."

"So you'll have to stay. You must be hungry. I'm sure Jennifer and Bill included you in the seating arrangement."

In fact, it was traditional to allow the wedding planner a seat at a back table. As Diana had coordinated the placing of seating cards on the tables, she knew exactly where her seat was.

"You must be hungry," Scott said. "Last night you had little to eat, and I'm sure you were at Jennifer's before breakfast. Have you had more than a cup of coffee today?"

She stared at him a moment, then shook her head.

"Stay. Give me one dance, and I won't bother you again today."

"Is that a promise?"

He raised his right hand in the Boy Scout salute. "I promise."

At that moment a procession of waiters came from several doors and made a ceremony of placing food in front of the guests. The smell of an old-fashioned kitchen reminded her that she was hungry. Scott was right about her food intake. Leaving without eating was running away from him, and she didn't want him to know how much he controlled her actions.

"I will have something to eat."

"And a dance," he prompted.

"One dance," she said. "One only."

His smile broadened, satisfied that he'd won the argument. Taking her arms impulsively, he pulled her forward and dropped a kiss on her cheek. Heat poured through her. Scott started back to his seat. Diana checked to see if anyone had seen the unexpected gesture. It was not protocol for the wedding planner to act as a guest or to be kissed on the floor of the dining room. But then Scott either didn't know the rules or didn't care to follow them. Jennifer and Bill were totally engrossed in each other. No one at the head of the room noticed. However, several people at the table close to where they stood smiled at her.

She nodded to them and quickly walked to her assigned seat. What was she going to do now? She couldn't possibly eat anything and keep it down. Thoughts of Scott pressing his body against hers in a dance was too much to think about. She was sure if he took her in his arms in the broad light of a beautiful sunny afternoon, she could not say she had no feelings for this man without the world around her knowing she was lying.

Chapter 4

Relax, Diana told herself as Scott whirled her about the room. She stepped on his foot once. He didn't say a word about it, didn't tell her to relax, didn't tell her he wouldn't bite, only adjusted his arms and pulled her close to him. Diana smelled his cologne. It was mildly sweet with an undercurrent of something that seemed to come from him. She liked it.

His head touched hers, and she closed her eyes. Her body relaxed and found the perfect combination of movement. She felt everything about him, the fabric of his starched shirt, the heat of his body beneath it, his long legs, and the sureness of his hands as they held her.

Being there was like a dream, and for a moment Diana allowed herself to fantasize that she was the bride dancing her first dance with her newly minted husband. Her feet seemed to glide across the floor.

The music stopped and she opened her eyes.

"That was beautiful," Jennifer said. "I've never seen anyone dance the way you two did. You make a beautiful couple."

Diana's skin burned. She hadn't realized she was being watched. Apparently, the entire room was staring at them.

What had she done? She knew. She'd fallen into the dream and let everything she felt pour through the dance. Hadn't she thought about that? She knew it was what many professional dancers wanted, strove to show on the stage. They wanted to show their feelings through the steps. Diana hadn't.

"Thank you," Scott said, saving her from having to answer anything. "I think we need a drink now."

He led her away from the prying eyes and toward the bar. The conversations resumed behind her, and she was certain that people had stopped staring at her.

"I apologize," Diana told Scott. "I never meant to embarrass you."

"You've danced before," he stated, apparently out of context. "And I'm not embarrassed."

Diana had taken lessons and learned many dances that couples used for their first dance. Often she needed to school the groom on a few steps before he took his bride onto the dance floor. At the time she viewed it as part of her full service to the wedding program. Today she regretted ever knowing a single step. Or the feel of Scott's arms holding her, almost cradling her as they traversed the floor.

"But people thought we were…" She stopped, unwilling to finish the thought.

"Thought we were what?" Scott asked.

"It doesn't matter," she said. "Whatever they thought, we're not."

"Are you sure? I can't imagine you've danced that way before."

"I may have." She took affront to his assumption, but knew she had never lost herself in a man's arms on a public dance floor.

"Then why did the color creep under your skin when Jennifer said we looked good together?"

"I'm not used to being the center of attention," she said.

"Then maybe we should get you a drink." They joined the line for the bar.

"And I'm not exactly your type."

"Type?" His brows rose. "I have a type?"

"You did once, and that usually doesn't change with age." She looked at the ceiling for a moment. Then back at him. "At college you majored in female anatomy. I don't believe I ever saw you with the same coed twice. Except for that one woman who followed you everywhere. What was her name?"

"Linda."

"Linda." Diana snapped her fingers as if the name had just come to her.

Scott listened carefully, saying nothing and only changing his expression to take a bite of his dinner or to drink from his glass.

"Your type was the leggy, long-haired, big-boobed girls. While most of us wore jeans and T-shirts to class, your women sported short skirts. The shorter, the better."

Scott nodded. "I don't believe I ever saw you with anyone. You were always alone. Neither male nor female satisfied your friendship."

"You're wrong. I had friends."

"Really?" His brows rose.

"Who?"

"I doubt you would know any of them. They didn't run in the same circles as you and your friends. They were the nerds."

"Everybody at Princeton was a nerd. It's an admission requirement."

Diana moved a step up and Scott bumped into her. "You consider yourself a nerd?"

"On good days. What do you consider me?"

"BMOC, hands down."

Scott smiled. He'd been a campus sensation and he knew it. Even if he hadn't been on the swim team, where every woman in school could ogle his phenomenal body, he would have been known for his devastating good looks. Diana was no exception. She'd sit in the back at swim meets and watch him, too. Then she'd leave just before he got out of the pool and started talking to the many women calling his name from the gallery.

They'd reached the bar. "White wine and a glass of ice water," he ordered. The bartender filled the order, and Scott handed the water to Diana.

"I want the wine," she said.

Scott took a sip. "I'm not driving. And you are. Wine and cars don't mix."

"I hardly think one glass of wine will impair my driving, but I won't argue." Diana knew she could handle a glass of wine, but the stress she'd been under the last few days, along with an impromptu trip to Montana and missed hours of sleep, she knew she probably should stick to water. Taking a sip, she looked up and several members of the wedding party heading for them. They acknowledged her and began talking to Scott.

Diana took the opportunity to slip away. Once outside, she practically ran to her van and was out of the driveway before Scott had a chance to stop her retreat. She promised him one dance. Promised and fulfilled. She didn't need to wait for his friends to criticize her for the past or to gape at how much her appearance had changed. She could say a thing or two about the change in them. And it would be less flattering.

Scott's sister's voice broke the silence as he entered his apartment later that evening. He ran for the phone, grabbing the receiver just as she clicked off. Piper always tried his home number first. He pulled his cell out, ready for it to ring when the light on his answering machine started to glow.

Pressing the button, he listened to Piper's deep alto tones as she asked about the wedding and if he'd met anyone interesting. Scott smiled at her comment. She was almost as bad as a mother wanting a grandchild. Piper had been married twice, divorced once. While she had no children yet, she wanted them, and each time she called, Scott wondered if she would tell him she was pregnant.

He checked his cell as he listened. It remained silent, but her voice said, "You're probably still at the reception or you got lucky, so I won't interrupt you by ringing your cell. Talk to you soon."

He heard the click when she disconnected. He and Piper were close. They had always been both friends and siblings. She understood him, but he knew the real purpose of her call was to test his attitude. She knows his buddies would rib him for being the last bachelor. He'd avoided the ribbing last night by ditching most of the bachelor party. But he couldn't skip the wedding or the reception.

They cornered him at the bar and Diana had gotten away. Almost the moment she was out of earshot, the conversation started on him settling down.

Then the matchmaking began. Women didn't think men tried to set other men up, but they were wrong. Even if men weren't looking for a long-term relationship, they wanted someone to have fun with. If that fun morphed into a relationship and then into something more, all the better.

"Where's that woman you were making love to on the dance floor?" asked Dan, a linebacker-size friend who never held his tongue.

"We weren't doing that," Scott said, feeling he needed to defend the absent Diana.

The guys laughed.

"She's a beauty. You could do worse," Steven put in. "But since she's gone, the woman I accompanied down the aisle does simultaneous translations. She works at the United Nations."

"Are you trying to set me up again?"

"You're not getting any younger," Steven said.

"I'm thirty-two, not sixty-two."

"And you fly around the country, not stopping long enough to spend a night in one place."

"I spend plenty of nights here."

"Are any of them with her?"

Dan's question had them all staring at Scott, waiting for an answer. While there was noise in the rest of the room, the small circle where they stood was a bubble of silence.

"Kiss and tell," Scott finally covered. "You think I should do that?"

"Yeah," Mike answered.

"We're no longer in college, guys," Scott reminded them.

"College," Mike said. "Was she…" He stopped. "No… she's not." He looked both surprised and incredulous.

"What are you trying to say?" Dan asked.

"Brainiac?" Mike's eyebrows rose. "Diana 4.0?"

"Who's Diana 4.0?" Dan asked.

"Tell me that's not her?" Mike addressed Scott. He looked over his shoulder in the direction Diana had gone.

"That's her," Scott said.

"Oh, man." Mike spun all the way around, giving a hoot and doing a little backward dance. "Whoever would have thought you and Diana 4.0 would have anything in common?"

"I'm lost," Dan said. "Who is she?"

"She was the brain in college," Mike explained. "Wow, the difference in appearance is almost indescribable. At school she had all this hair covering her face. Some of the guys on campus called her Cousin Itt."

Dan and Steven laughed. Scott didn't.

"Her nose was always in a book and our friend Scott here taunted her to no end. She hated him," Mike went on. "And you had no love for her, if I remember right."

"I remember her now. How did you two get together?" Steven asked.

"We're not together," Scott denied.

Dan looked at the dance floor. "I think there's a permanent groove out there where you two danced."

Scott knew he wasn't going to be able to explain this or live it down. Even Jennifer had remarked on his behavior on the dance floor with Diana. The problem was he hadn't been conscious of it while it was happening. If it was just his friends ribbing him, he could endure it, but Jennifer wasn't part of the group. She was Bill's wife now, but she didn't have the same history with them.

"What about Dorothy?" Steven asked.

All eyes went to him. "Who's Dorothy?" Mike asked.

"She was my partner going down the aisle. From what I hear, she's works for an airline. That ought to be right up your alley, Scott."

"Yeah," Dan agreed. "You two could meet in different cities and—"

"Stop," Scott said. "If you guys will leave me alone, I'll find my own woman. And what if I don't? I won't be the only man in America who's unmarried and liking it."

Scott spoke with finality. He wanted this conversation to end. He and Diana had no relationship, despite the dance and the two kisses that his friends didn't know about. As he'd told her, she intrigued him. A computer had put them together, matched them on more than fifty points of interest. Never mind that they had hated each other in college or that she was the last person on the planet he'd think of as compatible. But she was the one and only name that came up after he put in his requirements.

Scott would let his friends think he and Diana came together as a result of Bill and Jennifer's wedding. Not that he'd looked for the perfect match and got Diana 4.0.

Scott sat down, telling himself she wasn't the one. She couldn't be, yet since their meeting in the coffee shop, she was constantly on his mind. And she brought back memories he thought he'd buried ten years ago. He'd kissed her on campus. It was a prank, at least it started that way, but somewhere in the infinitesimal space between their lips meeting, she'd gotten under his skin. He'd tried to fight it off, but in the darkness, where both demons and conscious thought is true, his mind knew the truth. He was attracted to Brainiac.

For ten years he'd wondered about that day. He wanted to find out if it was just a fluke or if her kiss was as sensational as he remembered.

And then he kissed her again.

And it was.

The last American bachelor. Scott smiled at the moniker, but there was no humor in it. His buddies had given him the singles treatment. He knew some of them could be jealous and were using him to cover their true feelings, but for the most part they were happy men. And happier after they found their true loves.

Scott wondered if he would ever find his. That had been the foundation that led him to Diana. How could it possibly lead him full circle to the one woman in the universe that he'd never considered as a girlfriend, let alone a life mate? He and Brainiac had nothing in common.

So why was he aroused by her? In college he'd taunted her, trying to get a rise out of the long-haired, studious coed. He'd gone along with the guys in teasing her because she was different. She always had her head in a book, and some of his friends called her Diana 4.0 because she had a perfect record. She graduated with a 4.0 average.

Scott shared only one class with her. She sat in the back and never uttered a word unless specifically called upon, yet she aced every test. She hid behind her mane of straight hair and avoided looking at anyone. Her hair remained just as long as it had in the past, but she no longer hid behind it. She wore it in curls that framed her face and showed off high cheekbones, dramatic eyes and a mouth that beckoned him like a heat-seeking missile. Who knew beneath that brain was a captivating beauty?

And Scott never expected her identity to pop up when he completed the online form. He filled in a general description of the woman he was looking for, then checked practically every criterion box: speaks several languages; plays one or more musical instruments; owns business; financially secure; drives a car; understands wine, high fashion and jewels. Knows architecture; has a sense of humor and excellent interpersonal skills. It was more like a job interview than a relationship form.

The MatchforLove.com service notice said he would get at least three compatible matches based on his answers. Scott clicked the submit button and waited while the computer churned through the electricity to access the database housed somewhere in the world. Of course, no address was listed. The small icon on the screen circled and circled until he believed the system had frozen. He'd chosen everything, so how could any one person fulfill all those requirements?

After watching it for several minutes he went to get a beer from the refrigerator. He snapped the top off and threw it in the trash, then took a long swig before returning to the computer. He heard the ping just as he sat down. "You have a match," the impersonal voice stated.

Then the screen began to scroll information. There was no picture, but almost everything he'd checked or required came back to him in astonishing color. At the end of the file was an email address and a flashing message that said, *Send an email.* Scott took an hour to decide to make contact.

And that led him to Diana Greer.

"Thanks, Edward." Diana smiled at the barista and took the two cups. As she turned to leave, Scott stood in front of her.

"What are you doing here?" she asked. She'd been coming to this shop since she moved to Princeton. Except for the day they were to meet for the first time, she'd never seen Scott in this place. Diana didn't want to give up her favorite coffee shop, but she also didn't want to take the chance of running into him on a daily basis.

"I came for coffee. He looked at the two cups she was carrying. "Unless one of those is for me."

Diana pulled back on the cups in case he reached to take one away. "One is for my partner, Teddy, and the other is mine." She glanced over her shoulder, then back at him. "The line is short. I'm sure Edward will get you whatever you want." She walked past him and out the door. Luck wasn't with her today, as it hadn't been since Scott returned to her life.

The office was too far away for her to walk. She had

to get to her car. Diana had parked in one of the few spots close to the shop directly across from one of the large churches on the main street.

"Do you want something?" she asked, sitting the two cups on the roof and opening the car door. "Besides coffee?"

"You drive a Porsche?" Scott's eyes roved over the car as if it were a sex object.

Diana stared at him from the driver's side of the red sports car. She supposed he expected her to have a small compact. After all, Brainiac should drive something sensible, shouldn't she?

"I'm impressed," Scott said, laughter tinging his voice.

"Didn't think I'd do it, right? You expected me to drive a compact, something small, nondescript, something that could fade as easily into the walls as everyone expected me to do. Maybe I should have a dull green mom-mobile, or at the very least an SUV?"

"I expected a company van, logo on the side, custom-wrapped in pink with ribbons. Who would believe Diana 4.0 drove a Porsche?"

"Maybe the world will end," she told him.

Scott walked from the back to the front of the car. Several times he raised his eyebrows and nodded, giving it his approval.

"I do drive an SUV, by the way," Diana told him. He finally took his eyes off the car to look at her. "It's not pink, nor is it wrapped in ribbons. When I have a wedding or need to cart around large items, I pull it down off its cinder blocks and put the tires back on it."

"I saw it in your profile. That's why I expected…something different."

"That's the second time you've brought my profile into question."

"I just wondered if everything in it was true."

"Why?" she asked.

"It sounds extraordinary," Scott said. "You speak how many languages?"

"Four," she threw at him from the opposite side of the car. "Would you like me to reply in one of them? Or all of them?"

"And you play at least one instrument."

Diana closed her eyes and took a long intake of air. When she opened them, she set the coffee in the car and slammed the door.

Coming around the car, she stepped onto the sidewalk. The action brought her close to him and her shoes made her nearly as tall. "Follow me," she ordered. "You want to know about my profile?"

"You're so busy," Scott said. "How could you possibly do everything stated there and run a business, too?"

"I have a partner," Diana said.

"Even with a partner."

Diana went up the steps of the church in front of her car. "Open the door," she said.

Scott did as commanded. Inside Diana headed to the sanctuary, going down an aisle she was familiar with. The church piano set in the front. Sliding onto the bench, she took no time to prepare, but lit right into a Chopin nocturne. As if it were a medley, she transitioned into Bach, Mozart and Paganini. Leaving the masters behind, she flawlessly moved on to Gershwin, Bernstein, Rogers and Hammerstein, and Cole Porter, and ended with Stephen Sondheim. Standing up, she stared him in the face.

She spoke in German. "Would you like me to translate?

"'I am exactly as represented. Everything in my profile is the absolute truth. I told no lies. How many did you tell?'" he translated for her.

"I see you speak German. How about Italian, Russian and Chinese?" Diana didn't wait for an answer. She turned on her heel and marched up the sanctuary aisle.

Scott caught her at the door and turned her to face him. "There is only one lie in my profile," he said.

"Which one?" she asks.

"This one." He pulled her into his arms and delivered a kiss that curled her toes. Diana thought that phrase was the stuff of books or movies. It wasn't a real condition. People's toes didn't curl. But hers did. Her arms went around him. This wasn't like the kiss at the wedding rehearsal. There they had an audience. Here there was no one. They were together and alone. His mouth took hers in the sight of stained-glass windows, vaulted ceilings and the polished wood of the entry hall. Diana didn't think of where they were. She didn't think at all. She felt. She let his mouth tease hers and sweep her deeply into a recess of pleasure that had her groaning with delight.

His arms tightened around her waist, pulling her so close to him that not even air couldn't escape between them. When Scott finally dragged his mouth from hers, she was weak and limp in his arms. Her mind was muddled, making it impossible for her to think straight.

Diana was totally undone by his action and her complicity. This was a different experience. She'd been kissed by him before, but this kiss was the no-holds-barred kind. Yet it held a promise. This was not the time or place to continue, but in the kiss, Scott told her there would be a continuum. She might want to end their relationship because of their differences, but their time line had changed in the last few seconds.

Backing away from him, she tried to control her breathing. It took several moments before she trusted herself to speak. "That wasn't in your profile," she said.

Scott gave her a look filled with fire and desire. Then he spoke in a voice that was low and sexy and contained the same promise of more to come. "It is now."

Chapter 5

"What the hell is going on out there?" Diana said, coming into the office. She would have slammed the door if it didn't have that compressed soft-close feature.

Outside several trucks were in the parking lot. A full crew of men with jackhammers were polluting the air with the sounds of their machinery as they tore up the asphalt. This was all Diana needed. On top of dealing with Scott first thing in the morning, her coffee was now cold. And he was using a new tactic to get her to move.

"Let's see," Teddy said from the doorway of the small kitchenette where they had a microwave, a coffeemaker, a refrigerator and a small table. She leaned against the entrance, one foot crossed over the other and her arms folded. "I take it the wedding yesterday didn't go well."

"The wedding went fine," she said with a little less vehemence in her voice than the initial declaration.

"Then what did our golden boy do to upset you?"

"He's not *our* golden boy."

"But he has upset you?" Teddy dropped her arms and came farther into the kitchen. The microwave bell rang and Diana popped the door open, removing the two cups.

"He showed up at Edward's while I was getting coffee."

"Is that all?" Teddy knew there was more to Diana's anger than she had said so far. Her partner was very perceptive. Their business had taught them that there was more a bride wanted than what her words said. And while Diana wasn't a bride, she hadn't relayed the entire story.

Taking a sip of the reheated coffee, they moved to Diana's office, where she told Teddy the entire morning's activities, including the kiss just inside the church door. "And then I find this in the parking lot." She raised her arm toward the inner wall on the side of the building where the cars were parked.

"We've weathered this before," Teddy cautioned her. "This extreme reaction from you over a man is unusual."

"It's like he baits me," Diana said. "One minute he's Sir Galahad and the next he's the Grinch who stole Christmas."

"Why do you think that is?"

"I don't know. He acted like this when we were in school together. I was always the butt of his pranks. Any chance he had to embarrass me, he'd take it."

"How long have you been carrying this torch?"

Diana's head snapped up. She stared directly at her partner as if the other woman had suddenly begun speaking a foreign language.

"I am not attracted to him."

"This is me…Teddy." She placed a hand on her chest. "You can't lie to me."

That was all she needed to say. Diana dropped her shoulders and set her coffee cup on the desk.

"Damn," she said softly. Then she answered honestly, "Since my first day at college. I came out of a building and literally walked into him." She paused. "Since that day, he's only looked at me in order to belittle and ridicule."

"Don't worry," Teddy soothed her. "They say admission is the first step."

"Toward what?" Diana snickered. "A cure?"

"There is no cure for love." Teddy spoke the words as if they were a prayer.

"I'm not in love with him," Diana denied.

The two women stared at each other for a long moment. A smile raised the corners of Teddy's mouth, then grew wider. She began to laugh. Diana tried to hold it in, but Teddy's face broke into a smile that had Diana joining her. The smile grew until she was laughing. Diana tried to stop it, but only managed a hiccup and then a burst of sound. Suddenly both women were laughing as if they'd discovered the funniest thing on earth. Diana's eyes misted and she put her hand up to cover her mouth. The laughter grew until both women were dabbing at the corners of their eyes and the pent-up stress was released.

Diana could resort to only one method of getting through the days—work. She threw herself into the sale and management aspects of the business like a woman possessed.

By midmorning, she had read several reports that had piled up on her desk while she'd worked on the Embry wedding. She'd gone through her email and answered several phone calls. She updated the PowerPoint presentation she used when making an initial call.

As noon approached, her computer made a specific sound she hadn't heard in weeks, alerting her to a message from someone at MatchforLove.com. Diana's stomach clenched. She reached for her cell phone. The email address was familiar. The phone slipped from her fingers. She fought and caught it. There was a time when seeing that address caused excitement to race through her. Today it caused pain. She was not going to that site to collect a message. Her previous adventure with Scott ended in disaster. She wouldn't start it again.

Taking her leather pad emblazoned with the Weddings by Diana logo on it, she went to Teddy's office. They usually had a meeting on Monday morning. And it was still morning. At least for the next half hour.

Sitting down, she asked, "How are we set for the next month? Do we need any help?"

As usual, Teddy opened the schedule on her laptop and swung the screen around so they both could see it. There were five weddings in July.

"Can you handle them all?"

Teddy nodded. "There are several apprentices nearly ready to fly solo."

Diana didn't miss her partner's careful choice of words. Teddy was grooming the apprentices to lead, stepping in if needed, or if the bride was someone like Jennifer Embry, old money and difficult.

"Looks fine," Diana said.

"Everything's under control. What about the franchises?" Teddy asked.

Diana smiled. "I've had several calls this morning. Packets are going out. And the one in Montana is coming along. I think they'll be up and running by the end of the month."

"Any more trips out there?"

"Not at the moment, but I'll need to be there when the doors initially open."

At that moment the phone rang in the outer office. "Oops, that's me," Diana said, recognizing the ringtone.

"I'll get it." Teddy lifted the receiver and punched the button to reroute the call. "Weddings by Diana," she said. "This is Ms. Granville."

She listened to the caller. Diana read Teddy's face. It changed from surprise to a wide smile that relaxed her features. Diana wondered who it was. She thought it was someone inquiring about a franchise or a wedding. Then it sounded personal. She got up to leave, but Teddy waived her back.

Removing the receiver from her ear, Teddy offered it to Diana. "It's for you."

"Who is it?" Diana asked, taking the phone. From Teddy's expression and familiarity, it was obviously someone they knew outside of the business world.

"Scott."

Diana nearly dropped the tan-colored instrument. She put her hand over the mouthpiece. "What does he want?" she whispered.

"Only one way to find out," Teddy smiled.

Diana made a guttural noise in her throat and lifted the phone to her ear. "This is Ms. Greer," she answered formally. "How may I help you?"

"I apologize," Scott replied.

Diana expelled a long breath. If she was honest with herself, she'd admit it wasn't all his fault. Maybe Teddy was right and he was no longer the bane of her existence as he had once been. To punctuate his point the jackhammering outside flared loudly.

"Apology accepted," she said. "Is that all?"

"Not exactly."

"Well, what else is there?"

"Have dinner with me tonight?"

"Dinner?" Diana glanced at Teddy, who leaned forward in her chair, her head bobbing up and down in agreement. "I don't think so. We only seem to rub each other the wrong way."

"That's just it. I want to prove all the hostility is behind me."

"And you think dinner will do that?" Diana didn't try to hide her skepticism.

Teddy was grinning now. *Say yes,* she mouthed silently. Diana turned away from her.

"It may not be the total answer, but it's a start." His voice sounded sincere, but she wasn't convinced.

"Are you trying to get me to go to dinner so you can bring up the offices?"

"I would not do that. This is purely a friendship dinner."

"We're not friends," she told him.

"But we could be."

"I have too much work that piled up while I worked on the Embry wedding. I don't think—"

Teddy came around the desk and took the phone. "She'd love to go to dinner," Teddy answered. "What time?"

Diana grabbed for the phone, but Teddy eluded her. "Seven o'clock will be fine."

"I can't go," Diana said through clenched teeth.

"You can pick her up—"

"—at the office." Diana grabbed the phone, but Teddy held on tightly. She could only speak loudly into the mouthpiece. She didn't want Scott in her home. After the kiss in the church this morning, she didn't trust herself alone with him and in private.

"I'll see you at seven."

"Bye," Teddy said and replaced the receiver.

"Why did you do that? Why did you set me up with the one man I don't want to see?"

"Because he's the one man you *do* want to see." She gave Diana a pointed look. "And as my mother used to say, face the issue and get it out of your system or get it in your system."

"I don't have time for him. We've got weddings in the works. And that's where my attention should be."

"Learn to multitask," Teddy said.

The noise in the parking lot ceased around 4:00 p.m. Diana's headache kept going. Teddy usually worked late, but today she thought she'd leave early. Diana insisted that she remain until Scott arrived. Since she'd gotten Diana into this mess, she could well stay until the last possible moment. If this was a Victorian wedding, Diana could insist she act as chaperone. But they were more than a decade into a new century, and Diana and Scott already knew each other. A chaperone wouldn't be necessary. Maybe a referee was what they needed.

Both women watched from the office window as Scott got out of his car at two minutes before seven. He'd been impressed with Diana's Porsche. The car he got out of was a sleek red Lexus with vanity tags bearing the word FLYYBOY.

"He's punctual," Teddy said.

Diana's throat went dry. She watched him walk toward the glass doors. He wore khakis and a dark blue shirt, open at the neck. Even from here, the man was devastatingly attractive. He no longer sported the boyish steps of an emerging adult. He was all male, confident, sure of himself, and Diana knew how she could melt in his arms. Tonight she had to keep a lock on her emotions and make sure this morning was not repeated.

"All right, I've fulfilled my part. I'm going home." Teddy had her purse on her shoulder and was ready to leave. "Have a great night," she said. "Tell me all about it tomorrow."

"I will, and one day I hope to return the favor." Sarcasm tinged her voice.

She could hear Teddy's laugh as she headed down the hall toward the rear entrance. Her car was parked next to it, and she always said good-night to the guard who was stationed there.

Diana didn't try to stop her. From this point on, she was on her own. She could either act like a professional or she could fall over Scott like a lovesick schoolgirl. She was determined that the former happened and the latter was held in check.

Meeting him at the door, Diana unlocked it and slipped through. "I'm ready," she said. "Where are we eating?"

"I didn't know you'd be that hungry, or I'd have made the reservation for earlier."

She wasn't hungry at all. She didn't want to go to dinner. She didn't want to be in Scott's company, but she was committed.

"You look great." His eyes swept her up and down, looking admiringly at the white skirt and green off-the-shoulder sweater she wore. Unsure of their restaurant, she wore something that would work at most places in the area.

"Shall we go?" she asked.

He nodded. Diana locked the office door and they took the elevator to the ground floor. He'd parked next to her Porsche, but opened the door to his Lexus and helped her inside before walking around the hood to get in himself.

"About this morning," she said as soon as he was seated.

"Let's not talk about this morning," Scott said. "Let's enjoy the night."

Diana wasn't sure if she should press the point. She didn't know what she really wanted to say, only that something needed to be said. Some explanation needed to be rendered to set things straight. She decided against trying to find the words. The air between them was already heavy.

Scott drove through the narrow streets. At this hour a long, dark line of late-model cars was parked along the curb. Even for a Monday the population of the tiny hamlet was out in force. After circling Palmer Square, Scott pulled into a garage and shut down the engine. When he helped her out of the car, Diana immediately dropped the hand she held, but not before an electric current went up her arm.

The night was warm, and they walked the short distance to the center of town.

"I suppose if we don't talk about this morning, we have nothing to talk about," Diana said. "What happens when we get to the restaurant? We sit there looking at our food until the meal is over and we can go home?"

Scott stopped on the square leading up to Nassau Street, which was relatively empty. The small park in the center acted only as a causeway allowing cars to make a U-turn without traveling the full distance around the square.

"You want to talk about this morning?" His voice was harsh. "I'll tell you about it. The kiss was unintentional, but I enjoyed it. I thoroughly loved having you in my arms, having my mouth on yours, feeling the softness of your skin and smelling your morning soap and perfume. It was tantalizing, and despite the fact that we stood in a church, I wanted to take you right there and then."

Diana's back was to a wall. Scott was close enough for her to smell the minty toothpaste he'd used. She could move sideways in either direction, but his words pinned her to the spot.

"Is that what you wanted to hear?"

She swallowed. She didn't know what she wanted to hear, but his words had her heart singing. Did she really have that much of an effect on him? And so fast. How long had it been since they reconnected in person? A few weeks. In that time they'd shared two kisses, but they were constantly thrown in each other's path.

"Don't you have anything to say?" Scott asked. His voice wasn't as strong as it had been.

"Truthfully, I don't know what I wanted to hear. I wanted to know why you kissed me. We both know we have no future, yet twice now you've kissed me."

"Twice now, we've kissed each other," he corrected.

He moved in even closer to her. Diana tried to move back, but she had no place to go.

"Don't think I don't know you enjoyed it, too. You were right there, clinging to me, giving as good as you got."

Diana dropped her eyes for a moment, then looked back at him. "I admit it. I did like being kissed."

"By me," he challenged.

"By you," she said. "But don't take it to mean this is the beginning of anything, because it's not."

For the longest moment he stared into her eyes. She challenged him, refusing to look away no matter how much she wanted to. Scott was too close. Diana hoped he wouldn't move the half inch that would meld their mouths together. Her heart hammered in her head, and she battled her lungs to keep her breathing even. After what seemed like a century, Scott took a step back. She forced herself to exhale slowly. She didn't want him to know how long she'd been holding her breath and how hard she was trying to control her heartbeat. And, worse, how much she wanted him to kiss her again. Yet she was afraid he might.

They were only steps away from the entry gates of Princeton University and the expansive knoll of grass and walkways where Scott had first kissed her. It was a prank, a dare, and she knew it, but the result was the same as what had happened in church that morning. She was putty in his arms. He'd nailed her on it. She had no control when it came to him.

"Why don't we go on to dinner or you can take me back to my car? It seems our evening is ruined."

"One question."

She waited, again holding her breath at whatever Scott planned to say.

"What did you feel this morning?"

Diana pursed her lips and stared straight into Scott's eyes. He looked at her steadily. She wanted to know what he was thinking, but he gave her no clue of his expectations. Searching for something to say, she came up with nothing.

"I spend a lot of time working," she finally said. "It's been a long time since anyone kissed me or held me."

Scott let out a slow breath.

"I already admitted that I liked being kissed." She paused, taking a moment before going on. "Hate me now, but you could have been anyone. It wouldn't take much for me to find comfort in a man's arms."

She raised her eyes expecting him to be angry, waiting for the color to flood or drain from his face. Knowing his eyes would darken and he'd walk away, leaving her alone on the sidewalk. Secretly, she wanted it to happen. She could already see him going.

But it didn't.

Scott's eyes darkened but with need, not anger. He stepped forward. Her back was already against the retaining wall of an office building, and she found it solid and unmovable. She was trapped, both by the environment and by the man. Scott leaned close to her, so close his lips were only a millimeter from hers. She could taste his toothpaste. Emotions, wild and passionate, rocketed through her, and it took a superhuman effort for her to remain still.

She felt his mouth move on hers as he uttered one solitary word.

"Liar."

Chapter 6

The only good thing about their meal together was entering the restaurant. Because Diana worked with many caterers, she knew most of the restaurateurs in the area. They loved to see her, and she always got the best cuts of meat and the best prepared meals.

But while the food was excellent, she tasted nothing. Both she and Scott spent the meal avoiding looking at each other. Their conversation was stilted, cloaked in an atmosphere as thick as a white sauce. Diana was relieved when it was over. All she wanted was to get back to her car and away from the strain of a situation that should never have existed.

Yet when they were on the street and walking back toward the Square, Scott stopped at the light and looked toward campus, away from the place where the night had begun.

"What are you doing?" Diana asked, her voice low and tentative.

"Let's go for a walk," he said. Taking her hand, he didn't give her time to refuse but pulled her across the street and through the entry gates of the university.

"How was your time here?" he asked.

Diana slipped her hand from his. "Why do you want to know?"

He looked at the stars in the clear sky, then back at her as they walked across the pathway told the arch. "I just wondered. We kidded you a lot. I wondered how you felt about it."

"Now?" she asked. "You want to know how I feel all these years later?"

He nodded and stopped. Diana understood where they were standing. It was almost the exact spot where he had first kissed her. Where the kiss got out of control and he ran from her. She wondered if he'd stopped there on purpose or if he didn't remember the significance of this spot.

She moved away from it. She could see the girl she'd been, the one with the long, unruly hair and her nose in a book. The one who no one dated or even thought to ask out initially. She was a fish out of water on campus, and although she had many friends, it took a while for them to like her instead of only wanting her to help them with homework. These were people like her, smart but not part of the popular segment. Scott was a BMOC, Big Man on Campus. Everyone knew him and liked him. He always had a girl on his arm, and his crowd teased and taunted her. But it was Scott's zingers that hurt the most.

"For the most part, I enjoyed my years on campus," she finally answered. She felt safer talking about school than about their current relationship.

"What does that mean?"

"I know I wasn't part of your group. But I made a lot of friends while I was here." She looked at the university gates.

"I'm glad to hear that."

"Why?" Diana stood in front of him and stared in the

darkness. She couldn't see his full features, but the moonlight and the campus lights gave her a good enough view.

"I'm older now, and I don't like to think of the way I treated you when we were students."

"Are you apologizing?"

"I am," he said without hesitation. "It was the time and the group I was with."

"You're still with them. Wasn't Mike at the wedding?"

"He was surprised when he recognized you."

"Diana 4.0 or Brainiac? Although you were the only one who called me Brainiac."

"We were young and didn't think of how our words and deeds would affect others."

Diana resumed walking. The old hurt came back, but she refused to let him see it. "I'm a little older, too," she said. "I don't dwell on the things that were said and done then."

Scott took her arm and stopped her. When he noticed her glancing at his hand, he dropped it. "I am sorry," he said.

Diana could see it seemed important to him that she understand. His face was softer in the moonlight, and his anticipation seemed to hinge on her forgiveness.

"Thank you," she said.

It wasn't exactly an acceptance of an apology, but it was the best she could do. They gazed at each other for a while. The air around them took on a charge, and Diana knew she and Scott needed a buffer. She started walking. They continued to traverse the campus, as their hands met. She moved sideways to avoid contact. The silence between them stretched, and Diana felt that she should say something.

"We should go back," she told Scott. It was all she could come up with.

They turned and headed back toward the entrance. Diana wanted to go down a different path, avoiding the juncture where Scott had kissed Brainiac, but he steered her directly toward it. As another couple passed them, he entwined her arm with his and kept hold of her. Diana didn't wrench herself free of his touch. The feeling that came over her during their dance at the wedding was settling between them when Scott's cell phone rang.

"Damn," he cursed softly under his breath. Dropping contact with her, he pulled the phone from his pocket and looked at the display. He apologized and answered the call.

Scott listened for several seconds. "I'll be right there," he said and ended the call without saying goodbye. "I'm going to have to cut this short," he told Diana as he walked fast toward the exit. Scott said nothing about the caller or where he was running off to. "Let me get you a taxi."

"There are no taxis at this hour," Diana told him. They had reached the front gate. "I'll call Teddy to pick me up."

"Are you sure?" He stopped a moment to make sure she was all right with doing this.

"Of course," Diana said. "Go. Do what you have to. I'll be fine."

"I hate to leave you like this, but it is an emergency."

Diana took her cell phone from her purse. "Go," she said.

"I'll call you later," he said and took a couple of steps. His back was to her when the traffic light turned green. Scott didn't step off the curb. Instead, he turned back to her. In two steps she was in his arms and he kissed her. As quickly as it started it ended. He let her go and ran across the street down Palmer Square and disappeared around the corner. It was the same route he'd taken the day he'd kissed her on campus. It was night now and he was ten years older than he'd been that day, but Diana felt just as confused, uncertain and bereft as she had then.

Diana waited in the coffee shop across from the university. The place was full of jean-clad students, long-haired girls and guys with biceps the size of small trees. She looked out of place in her spaghetti-strapped dress and heels high enough to add five inches to her height. She hadn't wanted to call Teddy, but she couldn't walk in those shoes and calling anyone else would require too much explanation.

Through the glass window, Diana recognized Teddy's BMW. She gathered her small purse and giant cup of latte, which she rationalized she deserved, since Scott had left her stranded.

"You know, you two are going about this all wrong," Teddy said the moment Diana was seated. "You're supposed to be on a date. That's where the man sees you home and makes sure you're safely inside your house before leaving." She glanced sideways. "Or if you're lucky, he kisses you goodbye after breakfast. *Really* lucky would be breakfast, lunch and dinner."

"Obviously, my luck has run out," she said flatly.

Teddy was quiet for a moment. "What happened?" she asked as she navigated the streets.

"I don't know. We were walking on campus and he got a phone call. He explained it was an emergency and he had to go."

"He left you stranded here?" Her voice rose several notes.

Diana shook her head. "He didn't." She explained that she told him to go. That she would find her own way home.

"What was the emergency?" Teddy asked.

"I don't know."

"He didn't tell you?"

Again she shook her head.

"Was it female?"

"I don't know." Diana didn't want to answer any more questions. She didn't know anything, didn't understand what had happened.

"Do you think it was staged?"

"Staged?"

"Yeah, you know. When you aren't sure that you want to spend time with a person, you arrange for someone to call you at a specific time. Depending on your answer to the call, you either continue the date or you have a method of cutting the night short."

Diana came to that thought at the same time Teddy voiced it. She didn't want to believe it. Not after the way Scott had told her that he enjoyed their kiss this morning. And not after their walk through the university grounds. Or the final kiss.

"I don't think that was it," she said, but she wasn't sure. "Scott already knew who I was. If he didn't want to spend time with me, there was no reason for him to even ask me out."

"True," Teddy agreed, but her voice indicated she still had reservations.

"My car is still at the office. Take me there," Diana said, as Teddy turned down the street that would lead toward Diana's house.

"I don't think I should take you home. We should go to Winston's for a glass of wine. You can drown your emotions or at least dull them, and I could be the designated driver."

"There's nothing wrong with my emotions. I'd rather go home."

"This is Teddy, remember?"

"You said that this morning, before I got mixed up in all this."

"All right, it *is* partly my fault. I'm sorry I insisted you go to dinner with him. I never thought it would end like this."

Teddy pulled the car into a parking lot, but not at their office. She'd driven to Winston's, a local bar and restaurant not far from their office or the new hospital.

"What are we doing here?" Diana asked. Instead of answering, Teddy got out of the car, purse in hand, and closed the door. Diana could only follow. Even if she hadn't wanted to, Teddy took her arm and pulled her along.

"We're going to drown."

Scott set the plane down with barely a bump. He braked, bringing the huge bird to a slow speed before taxiing to the hangar. A medical team waited for him. The moment the fuselage doors opened they rushed into action. Within minutes an ambulance sped away, its lights flashing and sirens cutting the night air. Scott witnessed this scene many times and it never got old. He was helping to save someone's life, delivering transplant organs. He no longer asked for information about the patients, because he'd found that knowing compelled him to think about them rather than place his full concentration on flying. And in the air, mistakes were unforgivable.

As the lights of the ambulance faded he thought of Diana. Pulling his phone out, he headed for the hangar to call her. He got no answer on either her cell or her home number. He frowned, wondering where she was.

He'd left her abruptly. Without explanation. He didn't have time to tell her about the call. He knew that minutes could make a difference between life and death for someone. He had to go. His friends understood. Often he'd take a call and be gone without a word. But he wasn't sure she knew or understood.

Trying her number again, he was met with the same answering machine. Calling the office, a business voice that was unmistakably Diana's came over the line asking him to leave a message. Scott could hear the sexy undertone in it. Where was she? His flight had taken two hours after he got to the airport. It was nearly midnight in Princeton, and he knew she wasn't at a wedding tonight. So where was she? Had she reached Teddy? Had anything happened to her? Scott worried. Leaving a woman on the street wasn't like him.

Normally at this hour Scott would stay the night, but he was back in the air the minute the plane was refueled and serviced. It was three o'clock in the morning when he arrived in Princeton. Diana's car was still in the office parking lot, but there was no sign of her. Worry surfaced. Scott wished he knew Teddy's number. Or where she lived. Maybe she knew where Diana was.

At five o'clock in the morning Diana answered her landline. "This better be good," she said, her voice slurred.

"Diana?" He was surprised at the way she sounded, but relieved that she was home.

"Go away," she said.

"It's Scott."

"Scott, go away."

He was unsure if she was half asleep or ill. She sounded strange. "Diana, are you ok?"

"Go away," she said again. He heard the phone click in his ear. She'd hung up on him.

Something was wrong, Scott thought. He didn't like the sound of her voice. He redialed the number and started the car at the same time. She didn't answer. He didn't know how long it took him to get to her house, but it was less than it should have taken if he'd obeyed all the traffic laws.

Jumping out of the car, he was on her porch in a matter of seconds, his finger pushing and holding the doorbell. His mind imagined she was hurt, attacked, unconscious, unable to get to the door. He started knocking loudly and calling her name. Half a minute later, she opened the door a crack.

She pushed his hand off the bell. "Could you stop that noise?"

"You're drunk," Scott said. Still he was relieved.

"I am not drunk," Diana countered. "I was drunk, but I'm past drunk now. So go away."

Instead of leaving, he pushed the door open and walked inside. Diana lost her balance, her arms flailed as she tried to keep from falling. Scott caught her hand and pulled her upright.

"Maybe you better sit down."

"Maybe you better leave." Her hands moved in the air like she wanted to point at him, but couldn't find his image in the many she was seeing. If Scott hadn't been so relieved that she was only drunk and not hurt, he'd laugh. He moved her to the sofa and sat her down. "You left me at the altar."

"Where?"

"Where did the moon go?" She laughed. "I know...I know," she repeated. Then she fell sideways and passed out.

The groan Diana heard woke her. She felt terrible.

"Ugh." Her mouth tasted like copper. Raising a hand to her head, she pushed her hair aside. The effort hurt and she groaned again. What had she done? She tried opening her eyes, but the effort was too much. She squeezed them shut and found even that hurt. With a harsh moan she flopped back against the sheets. Something was behind her. This wasn't her bed. Where was she? Again she tried to open her eyes. Squinting, she peered through slits. What was she doing in the living room? And why was... *No,* she thought. Her brain was still soaked in wine. She thought she saw... But she couldn't have.

Diana tried to turn over, away from the light filtering through her eyelids. She fell. Her eyes opened wide. She was on the floor. She heard something. Then hands touched her. She jumped and began to fight.

"Stop it!" Scott shouted. "It's me."

Diana looked up, startled to see Scott staring down at her. She immediately stopped struggling. And closed her eyes. She had to be dreaming. But if she was, it was the first time she felt, really felt, hands. She opened her eyes again, then squinted. Pain shot through them, but not before she recognized Scott.

"What are you doing here?" Every word she spoke hurt her head. She put her hand up to it. Scott's hands were still at her waist and she was still lying on the floor.

"You don't remember letting me in last night?"

"I let you in?" Diana asked, raising her voice at the end making it a question.

"It's a good thing I'm an honorable man."

Diana levered herself up and sat with her back against the sofa. The effort took most of her energy. She needed to close her eyes, but forced them to remain open. "If you were honorable, you'd have gone home and let me wake up without anyone knowing how bad I feel."

Scott laughed. "Is this your first hangover?"

"Is that what this is? Why do people drink like this? My head feels like it will either fall off or explode."

"Why did you go drinking?"

"It was Teddy's idea. At least I think it was."

"Did she have something to drown?"

"Me," she said.

"Why you?"

Her head was clear enough that she knew better than to answer. "I'm all right now. You don't have to babysit me."

"You owe me a walk," he said.

"I owe you nothing. I completed the walk—*alone*." Her voice wasn't strong enough to prevent the pain the word evoked, but she endured it.

He stood up and pulled her to her feet. For a moment she was unsteady and clung to him. She still wore the dress she'd had on last night, but she had no memory of getting home or falling asleep on the sofa. Where was Teddy, and why wasn't she the one who stayed the night?

"Did you see Teddy?" Diana asked.

"Not today."

Diana, feeling strong enough to stand on her own, pushed herself out of Scott's arms. Then realizing her mistake, she sat down on the sofa and fell sideways, gathering a pillow she hugged it to cushion her head.

"I need something to drink. Would you get me a bottle of water?"

"That's the last thing you need," Scott told her.

"Why?"

"It'll make you drunk all over. Got any tomato juice? I'll make you a hangover cocktail."

"Too much salt," she said with a frown.

Scott disappeared. Diana tried to go back to sleep. At lease there she wasn't in pain.

"Diana?"

She heard her name called, but didn't want to answer. Answering caused pain.

"Diana?"

"Go away," she muttered, turning her head away from the sound.

"Turn over and drink this. It'll make you feel better."

She wasn't sure she believed him, but her head hurt so bad, only death would make her feel better. She heard Scott sit a glass on the coffee table. The sound of the glass rang like a loud bell. The seat next to her depressed as Scott sat down on the sofa. His body was hot next to hers. Hands took her shoulders and turned her gently. She faced him.

Picking up the glass, he offered it to her.

"What is it?" she asked.

"Orange juice and a few ingredients from your refrigerator and cabinets. Don't ask, just drink."

Lifting her head off the sofa, Scott supported her and held onto the glass while she drank.

"Yuk," she said. "It tastes like Drano."

"Drink it all," he ordered, pressing the glass to her lips.

Diana did as she was told, then let her head fall back against the sofa pillow.

"Fresh air is the next best thing," Scott said. "Come on. We'll go for a walk."

"Walk! I don't think I can stand, let alone walk."

Scott levered her to her feet. "You can lean on me."

She stepped sideways, testing her ability to stand alone. "I need to change clothes."

"Can you do it alone?"

"Of course, I can." She wasn't sure if that was true. She could get out of her dress and into pants and a shirt. It was getting to the second floor that posed a challenge. She took a tentative step, grabbing the newel post and closing her eyes. Nausea threatened, and she waited until it passed. She got to the fourth step and stopped. A moment later she made it the rest of the way. At the top, she headed to the bathroom to brush away the taste of last night's alcohol as well as whatever Scott had given her.

Diana felt no better returning to the living room, but she was dressed in more appropriate clothing for walking. She couldn't explain why she went with Scott. After he left her standing on the street corner last night, she shouldn't even be talking to him.

Scott led her to the door and turned to her. "You might want to get some sunglasses," he suggested.

Even with the glasses, the sun was strong. Scott offered Diana his arm, and she had to take it. She was unsteady on her feet and constantly closing her eyes against the glaring pain. Scott took the lead, deciding where they walked and how they got there. After a while she realized they were in the center of town near the campus buildings that had dominated Princeton for more than two centuries.

"What are we doing here?" Diana asked. "I didn't realize we'd walked so far."

"That's a good thing. You must be feeling better," Scott said.

Or going blind, Diana thought, but didn't voice it. Her head pounded, but the ringing in her ears was gone, and the traffic along Nassau Street no longer sounded like a cacophony of poor-quality steel drums.

They wandered toward Blair Arch. It was a meeting place, home of several choruses, and a natural division between upper and lower areas of campus. When they reached it, Diana stopped. She took a seat on the steps facing the lower campus and let the shade soothe the pain in her head.

"You asked me if I enjoyed my time here," she said.

"And you said you did." Scott looked over the area, sitting next to her.

"What about you?" she asked. "Did you enjoy being a student here?"

"I did," he finally said, but his voice conveyed something else.

"What's wrong? You sound like you didn't really like it."

He looked over the campus in front of them. Green lawn spread out like a carpet. Diana wondered if he was seeing the young man he once was.

"It was a long time ago," she told him, soothing whatever it was that appeared to haunt him.

"I wish I could go back and change some things."

"What would you want to change? You had everything. You were a BMOC. Everyone knew you. Everyone liked you. There was always a girl trying to get your attention."

"All except one." He looked directly at her when he said that. His voice was quiet as if they were in a library or one of the campus chapels.

"Me? You didn't want my attention."

"I would have changed how I treated you," he said.

"I don't think about it. It was a lifetime ago. I'm no longer the girl who went to school here. I'm older, hopefully wiser." She smiled, trying to lighten the mood.

"Don't you feel something every time you pass by?"

"Feel what? Envy. Pride. Hostility? My memories are good ones. You might not know it, but you and your group weren't the only people I met as a student. It isn't the campus that causes memories." She left the unspoken sentence hanging in the shaded air. "The ground and buildings are just that. The people are gone."

For long moments they were quiet, each lost in their own thoughts. In college Diana had watched Scott and his friends from afar. While they played with a Frisbee on the campus lawn or gathered in a hall, she'd had to study extra hard to keep her scholarship and work for extra money. She'd gone on a few dates, had friends, but there had been no one special in her entire college career.

"We'd better start back. It's a long way, and I feel better," Diana said.

They got up. Scott took her arm when she appeared unsteady. He dropped it as soon as she was able to stand. They headed back toward the front gate.

"How's your head feel?" Scott asked as they began to walk.

"Better," Diana said. "Thanks for the walk and the medical advice."

"I've been where you are, many times." He smiled, apparently remembering past mornings-after.

Classes ended and the grounds were suddenly dotted with young men and women moving back and forth across the campus. Despite it being summer, classes were in session.

"You know, when I went to class here, I never walked through those gates." She indicated the main gate a few yards away. It wasn't a real gate, not one you could close to keep people either in or out. It was a passageway, two high brick pillars with stone lions atop them.

"Why not? You weren't superstitious, were you?" Scott stepped off the path allowing a couple walking hand in hand to pass them. The girl smiled at him. Many students felt that walking through the gates meant they would never graduate, so they avoided the use of them.

"I wasn't superstitious. It's just that there was always a lot of activity going on here," Diana said. "I was forced to go another way."

"You mean we were out here playing. And you were avoiding us," he accused.

"Not all the time," she said. "I didn't intentionally avoid you and the others. But now, I always come in this way."

"You stage weddings here?"

Diana laughed. "I'm on the alumni board and usually park on a side street. Going in that way is more convenient."

Silence settled over them as they approached the spot in the walkway that Diana thought of as the kissing place. She didn't stop there, but passed it.

"Do you mind if I ask a question?" she asked.

He turned and looked at her inquiringly.

Teddy's comment that he might have arranged the call to cut their time together short was on her mind. But if he had, it made no sense. Why would he stay the night with her if there was another woman he wanted to see?

"Where did you go last night in such a hurry?" Diana asked.

"I had an emergency flight to take."

"I thought you were a corporate pilot," Diana said.

"Even corporate pilots have emergencies. But I'm not strictly a corporate pilot."

Diana waited for further explanation.

"I fly corporate executives from Centex Biologics. In addition, I sometimes deliver human organs for transplant."

"Transplants." Diana was relieved. "This is what you did last night. You flew an organ to save someone's life?"

"I tried. I deliver the organ. I can't tell if the operation is successful or even if the recipient is male or female."

Diana lifted herself up on her toes and kissed him on the cheek.

"What was that for?"

"For being one of the good guys."

She didn't think anyone would make up that kind of explanation. Diana didn't know what she would have thought if Scott had decided to leave her alone after he'd invited her to have dinner with him. Diana wanted to go, but she wouldn't let Teddy or Scott know that was the case. She'd have refused Scott's invitation if Teddy had not taken the phone.

But all the tumblers had fallen in place and they were together. Dinner hadn't been all she wanted it to be, but the walk on campus had begun well enough. Then Scott left her, but he was saving someone's life. Of all the things she could fault him for, that wasn't one of them.

They resumed walking, this time Scott took her hand. Just as they were passing Nassau Hall, the main building seen from the front gates, a group of people exited the building. Most of them were students, but a few were faculty.

"Hi, Diana," Dr. Rhys-Weisz said.

"Hello, Diana," said her colleague, Dr. Lange. "There's no committee meeting tonight, is there?"

Diana shook her head. "I'm just showing a friend around." She glanced between Scott and Dr. Lange. "This is Scott Thomas," she said.

They shook hands, and the two teachers excused themselves to hurry along to class. Dr. Lange and Dr. Rhys-Weisz were on a committee with Diana.

"They didn't recognize you," Diana said, surprise evident in her voice.

"Why should they?"

"You don't know who they are?"

Scott watched the two people walking away from them. He cocked his head as if trying to pull a memory into focus.

"Wait a minute," he said. "That was Professor Lange."

"He got his doctorate a few years ago," Diana told him.

"And Dr. Rhys?"

"She got married," Diana supplied. She's Dr. Rhys-Weisz now."

"You know them?"

She nodded.

"How?" he asked.

Before she could answer, Dr. Rhys-Weisz called her name. "You are coming next Saturday, right?"

Diana nodded. "I wouldn't miss it."

"I'm amazed she's still here," Scott said as the teacher left. "We used to walk all over her."

"She's still here," Diana said. "And I guess she learned from you, because she's a force to be reckoned with now."

They continued to walk, and a few other people smiled and spoke to Diana by name as she and Scott approached the main gate.

"You seem to have a presence here."

She nodded, not explaining.

"Can I surmise that your memories of being here continue to form?"

"You can," she said with a bright smile.

"What's happening next week?" he asked. "If I'm not overstepping my bounds."

"A few people are coming in for dinner."

"You mean the alumni?"

"Of course, they're all alumni." Diana made light of the situation as if the event was no big deal.

"It's the annual scholarship dinner," Scott said. "I have an invitation at home."

"They were sent to all alumni," Diana said. "Most people don't appear in person. If they did we couldn't accommodate them. Many send donations. About three or four hundred people attend the actual event."

Scott had never been there as far as Diana knew. He made regular donations. She got the list of attendees and

patrons every year. Her first job on the dinner-dance committee was to send acknowledgments to the alumni who
donated to the fund. She hadn't looked for his name, but
it had jumped out at her like an unexpected snake.

"You're going?" he asked.

"I'm on the committee."

"How about we go together?" Scott asked. "You let me
make up for running out on you yesterday, and I'll make
sure I'm not on call next Saturday. This is not a major reunion. It's not likely they'll be many people there either
of us know."

"Then why do you want to go?" she asked. "Isn't the
point of a reunion to see people you haven't seen in a long
while?"

"I'm sure there'll be at least a few people I remember.
And since we're both right in Princeton, maybe we should
go together."

"Scott, the BMOC and Diana 4.0. *together.*"

Chapter 7

Scott's car blocked the driveway when the campus taxi dropped them off several minutes later. They had walked to the center of town to clear their heads. Traversing the distance back over small hills that looked like mountains was more exercise than she wanted.

"I'm hungry," Diana told him when they were inside. She headed for the kitchen. "Want some breakfast, or is it lunchtime?" She checked her wrist. It was bare. Her watch was upstairs on the bedside table. At least that was where she hoped it was. The events of last night were still a little fuzzy.

"I'd love some. Anything I can do to help?"

"Set the table and make coffee." She indicated where the coffee was and pointed to the coffeemaker.

Diana moved around the space with steps as precise as a dancer's. In just a few minutes they were sitting down to a full breakfast of British bangers, scrambled eggs, Nutella crepes and buckets of coffee.

They ate in companionable silence, enjoying the food, but when Diana finished and poured a second cup of coffee for herself, she leaned back in the chair and gazed at Scott. He was an enigma. She wondered how the two personalities could occupy the same gorgeous body. One of his personalities left her in the dark. The other spent the night making sure she was all right and then helping her through the worst day of her life.

"What are you doing?" Scott asked. He had another cup of coffee and she hadn't seen him get up to get it or even remove both their plates.

"I was thinking of something."

"Was it about me?" he said with a smile.

"As self-centered as ever, aren't you?"

He sipped the hot liquid and shook his head. "I just hoped I was the object of your thoughts."

"Good or bad?"

"Your expression said good, so I went with that."

Diana waited a long moment before she answered his question. "I don't know if it was good or bad."

"What?"

"Why did you kiss me that day?" Diana asked.

Scott's face didn't change, but she knew he understood she was referring to the kiss he'd given her in front of Nassau Hall and not the one last night before he'd left her. Whatever his reason was, it had bothered her for years. She wanted to put it out of her mind. She'd tried, but suddenly without notice, she would remember it.

Some days she would hear a voice that sounded like his, only to turn and find it belonged to a stranger. There were television actors who showed traits she remembered him having; the way they ran or drew a hand through their hair. When a movie got to a love scene, Diana would fantasize that the man was Scott and she was the leading lady. For a time she only watched plotless actions movies.

"When we were students," he stated, knowing exactly what day and what kiss she meant.

She nodded. "It was one of the only times you talked to

me without harsh words, without an audience. I thought you were changing. Then you kissed me. And you ran away."

"We had an audience." He lowered his head and looked at his hands. "It was a joke, another prank against Diana 4.0."

She listened without a word.

"They were in the window of the building behind us. We saw you coming across campus and someone said something about how you probably had never been kissed. Of course, the conversation quickly got out of control. And then they thought one of us should go out and kiss you."

"And you lost."

"That wasn't how it was."

He was silence for a while. She was about to prompt him when he began speaking again. "I liked my friends back then. I still like them. They're married now and settled, but at the time I was unsure what they might do if someone else tried to complete the bet."

"So your act was to save me?"

"It doesn't sound noble, and at the time I didn't think of it that way. I was just unsure what would happen if one of them tried something and you didn't like it."

"You thought I might hurt one of them?"

"I doubt you could have. You were so much smaller than any of them. And they were either basketball or football players."

"You were on the diving team, but just as strong as any of them."

"But I wasn't about to hurt you," he said. "At least not physically." The last he added in a lower voice.

"I remember you started talking about a class. It had something to do with political science. You mentioned joining a campaign and wanted to know what I thought of the current presidential candidates." Diana didn't relay all he had said. She could repeat that conversation word for word if needed.

"You were skeptical of my motives," Scott reminded her. "I remember the expression on your face and you asking me why I wanted to know anything."

"You said you were interested in running for office, and you wanted to know how to change someone's mind that you had offended. I was the perfect patsy for that."

Scott winced, remembering that long-ago conversation. He reached across the table and took her hand. "I'm sorry for that day."

"What do you think your kiss did?" Diana asked.

"I've wondered about that for years. I thought you'd forgotten it. That it meant nothing."

"Is that's why you ran away?"

He shook his head. "I was surprised," he admitted.

"That the kiss was not my first time?"

"That I liked it and every time I saw you I wanted to kiss you again. After that I never teased you again."

"I know," she told him. "And you must have convinced your friends, because most of them stopped, too. I thought they'd found another target, but I knew it was you."

"We didn't find another target. I think we grew up at that moment and realized what we were doing was something we wouldn't want done to us. All except Linda."

"She thoroughly doesn't like me. Her harsh criticism continued." It had actually stepped up a few notches after the kiss.

"I never understood that. What did you ever do to her?" Scott asked.

"Nothing," Diana said. "I existed, and she knew about the kiss and your abrupt exit." It was a woman thing, and Diana wouldn't reveal it to Scott. It would tell him too much about her. Linda instinctively knew that Diana was a threat to her—competition for Scott's affections. Once she found out Scott had kissed her and no longer wanted to tease her, Linda would know that deep down Scott felt something for Brainiac.

"Yeah," Scott said, as if Diana had asked a question. "So?"

"While your male friends didn't get it, Linda did."

Scott frowned. He still didn't know what she meant.

"I was a threat to her. She wanted to make sure that she had your full attention, that she was the woman on your arm and no one else would replace her."

"She thought you would replace her?"

Diana gave him a long look. "It wasn't a peck on the cheek. When you kissed me, we were both surprised at the intensity that overtook us. Your friends were watching, and they embellished what they saw. So she continued her waspish comments and her belittling of anything I did."

"Good thing she married and left the area," Scott said.

That came as a surprise to Diana. The way Linda clung to him, she was sure they would have gone down the aisle together. She wanted to ask what had happened with the two of them, but didn't.

"She's probably a lot different now," Diana told him, and left the sentence obviously unfinished.

"Yeah, we're all different."

Scott got up and reached over to Diana. He pulled her to her feet and circled her waist. "I'm going to kiss you," he said. "And this time I'm not running away."

Teddy had come through for her. Diana knew she would. After Scott offered to take her to the dinner-dance, she wanted to look good, but after they made love, she wanted to outshine any woman he'd ever been with. She wanted to obliterate Diana 4.0 and Cousin Itt from his memory and let him see that she was a sexy, flesh-and-blood woman. And her blood ran hot for him.

Diana needed a gown. "Not just any gown," she told Teddy. "I need a gown that says WOW! Something that will knock Scott's eyes out when he sees me."

"Gee, this sounds serious, and over someone you said you weren't compatible with," Teddy teased.

Diana's face crimsoned under her makeup, but she only smiled at Teddy. Diana knew the inner glow she felt was evident. *Not compatible.* All that had changed. It was never really true. Diana had given herself that excuse to keep from confronting the fact that she really liked Scott. She thought about him the moment she woke up and every minute throughout the day.

"I'll see what I can do," Teddy said.

And now they were together. The BMOC and Diana 4.0. And they liked each other. She smiled to herself as she looked in the mirror. The dress was superb, a strapless royal-blue concoction that looked like blooming roses along the bustline. It pinched tightly in at the waist before flaring out as it fell to the floor. Teddy called in a favor and in a week got a dress fit for a queen. She knew exactly what Diana wanted, and the drawing Teddy sketched lived up to Diana's expectations.

She was rewarded when Scott arrived to pick her up. When she opened the door, he stared at her openmouthed and speechless.

"Wow," he finally said, and she smiled.

Her hair was off her face, removing all traces of the Cousin Itt persona. This Diana bore no resemblance to the old Diana who moved about the Princeton campus. From looking at her, no one would know that Diana 4.0

resided under the ringlets of curls or inside a person who was dressed to kill.

The dinner was going well when they arrived. Before people sat down, there was a reception for mingling and renewing friendships. Diana was apprehensive. She knew some time during the night, someone was going to comment on the BMOC being with the 4.0. Scott supported her, even understood her feelings. No one seemed to notice anything unusual. She got a few appraising glances. Finally she relaxed, sipping her drink and smiling at some of the people she had once known who hadn't been at a dinner before. Many of them didn't recognize her and looked at her admiringly.

But her relaxation was short-lived. Her heart stopped when she saw the woman and realized the night was just beginning.

Diana recognized her as soon as she walked through the door. She was as gorgeous as she'd been when they were students. Marriage and divorce hadn't changed her God-given beauty. But the inner working that made a person beautiful from the inside was missing from Linda Engles, Scott's old girlfriend.

She stood in the doorway, searching for someone. Diana knew without asking who she was looking for. Gripping her drink tighter, she touched Scott's back.

"Scott," Linda called the moment he turned. Her steps were determined as she rushed across the room, making a line for him as if she'd only been to the ladies' room and was returning to their date.

Scott turned as did everyone else in the room. This was the way Linda liked it. She loved being the center of attention and would do anything to make sure all eyes were on her.

Linda went straight into Scott's arms and kissed him on the mouth. "Scott, darling, it's so good to see you again."

Scott pushed her back. "Linda," he said, surprised. "It's great to see you, too." His voice seemed a little embarrassed to Diana. Taking his handkerchief from an outer pocket, he removed her lipstick.

Scott put his arm around Diana's waist and pulled her close.

"This is Diana Greer," he introduced. "You remember her?"

"Oh...my...God," Linda shouted loud enough for the entire room to hear. "I don't believe it. What a *transformation.*" The tone she used said it was impossible. "What is she doing here?" Her question was directed at Scott.

"Diana is on the committee for this dance." Again his hand went to her back, settling just at the place where the zipper separated her bare skin from the fabric. "She runs a business now called Weddings by Diana."

Linda looked around at the crowd. Diana knew it was coming. If no one in the room realized who she was, Linda would make sure they all knew. And in the worst light. Scott tightened his arm around her and turned her away.

"We were about to get a drink. Excuse us." They took a couple of steps and Diana realized he was trying to work them to another part of the room. But obviously Linda was having none of that.

"Wait," she said. "This is Brainiac." She stepped forward and grabbed Diana's arm. "You guys remember her? Diana 4.0." Linda stepped back, placing both hands on her hips and inspecting Diana. "You're a Cinderella if I've ever seen one."

Diana heard the expelling of air as people remembered who she used to be. She leaned toward Linda and whispered only for her ears, "That means I get to go home with the prince."

Linda's face reddened then drained. Diana turned to the crowd and lifted her head with a large smile on her face. "You all probably remember me as the studious girl who always had her head in a book." A low giggle went through the room. "Well, I was a scholarship student, and I had to keep my grades up if I wanted to stay in school. So I'm glad you're all supporting the fund tonight. After all, there may be someone out there just like me. And look how I turned out."

Diana lifted her arms and twirled around. Thanks to Teddy and her contacts in the world of high couture, Diana was dressed to the nines. Her hair was swept up completely off her face in a ponytail of cascading curls that fell to the middle of her back. Her only jewelry was a huge sapphire teardrop necklace that was circled with tiny diamonds and matching earrings.

She heard the approval from the audience, especially the males in attendance. At one time, most of these now ex-classmates wouldn't speak to her except to ridicule her. Now they looked upon her as eye candy.

Scott came up beside her and took her arm. "Thank you all for coming," he said. "And don't forget. Be generous."

They headed for the bar. Linda Engles was left standing alone, clearly bewildered that her little attempt to embarrass Diana had backfired. Diana gave the other woman a pointed look and followed Scott.

"That was interesting," Diana said when they were seated at their table with fresh glasses of wine.

"When did she get back in town?" he asked another guest sitting with them.

"I don't know, but I hear she's divorced."

Diana glanced at Linda. Her back was to them. She

was speaking to another couple with animated, if not exaggerated laughter. But she already had her sights on Scott. Diana didn't tell him how apparent it was that Linda wanted to continue the relationship they'd once had. She couldn't say it was where they had left things, because she didn't know the circumstances of their parting. But from the way Linda wanted to tear Diana's eyes out, she was gunning for Scott and didn't think Brainiac was an obstacle. Little did Linda know that Brainiac had learned a thing or two and she wasn't ready to crawl into her dorm room and hide from any insults that might be inflicted upon her.

"I hope she's only here for the dinner," Scott said.

"Sorry, but the word in the ladies' room is she bought a house in Rocky Hill," a woman sitting across from Scott said. Rocky Hill was small town fifteen minutes north of Princeton.

"Let's hope she's learned something in the ensuing years and she won't let things get out of hand," Scott said.

"From the way she looked at you, I believe she wants to pick up where you two left off," Diana whispered.

"That's not going to happen," Scott said in a tone that had Diana staring at him. "It wasn't the best of times," he told her. "And what makes you think she's after me?"

"I'm not blind. It was obvious from the way she looked at you, gave you all her attention to the exclusion of the rest of the room."

She'd only glanced at Diana before she recognized her and then tried to resume her past association with Scott, using Diana as a punching bag. She probably expected Scott to do the same.

Thank heaven he'd been the attentive date. But Diana still wondered. Scott and Linda had been a couple for three years. They hadn't parted until after graduation. Diana moved to take a job and lost track of the two. She heard that

Linda had married a few years later, and was relieved to discover she had not married Scott. She didn't know where Scott was, and her business was getting started. All her energy went into it, and she didn't think about him until the day he walked into her office an hour after his lawyer left.

Now she was glad to be on Scott's arm. But whatever Linda wanted…Linda got.

And Linda wanted Scott. But so did Diana.

As soon as the dinner and the speeches ended, the dancing began. Scott led Diana to the floor and straight into his arms. The two circled the floor for several dances, keeping step to the music as they held each other for all to see. As soon as the band gave them a breather from all the fast-tempo songs and played something slower, Linda Engles made her move.

"You can't monopolize him all night," she said. "Scott, let's dance for old time's sake." Linda grabbed his arm and pulled him away, then pushed herself into his arms. Scott looked back at Diana, But Linda turned his head so he faced her.

Diana moved back, intent on going to her table, when Mike grabbed her arm. "Dance with me," he said, leading her to the floor. Without a thought the two began to dance.

"I see those two are back where they started."

Diana looked at Scott and Linda to make sure they were the couple he was referring to."

"She's only just back in town."

"Yeah," he said. "But she's got an agenda, and it's on the floor right now."

Diana checked the dancers. Sex on the floor was all she could think of when she saw the way Linda danced with Scott. Her gown was skintight. Every voluptuous curve she had was outlined in the shimmering gold fabric. Her body was so close to Scott's, Diana was sure no air was between them. It was a reenactment of their college days. If you saw Scott, you saw Linda. The two were so closely associated that people spoke of them almost as one name.

Diana scanned the faces of Scott's friends. Approving smiles showed white teeth and envy. She felt like the outcast. The best couple was on the floor, and few people remember the others. And Diana's name was never on anyone's list for any of the "most likely" awards. Linda and Scott, most likely to marry and have beautiful children. Diana, most likely to be forgotten.

But she hadn't let that stop her. She might be forgotten by Scott and Linda's crowd, but she was known well in her own circle. Her group of people were not superficial and interested only in themselves. They went on to become the quietly rich and famous in the background, not looking for the limelight. In many ways Diana could see in them the same qualities she found in the high-profile weddings she planned. They wanted quantity, not realizing that something of quality would add more elegance. While Linda might be dressed in the finest Versace had to offer, she still looked like a peasant. And Diana wasn't just being catty.

The dance finally ended, and the two went to get a drink from the bar. As soon as Scott handed a glass to Linda, he excused himself. Diana smiled. Her heart bloomed in her chest that he was forsaking Linda for her. Unfortunately, he was waylaid by his friends. Diana knew what they were doing. They were congratulating him on the dance. Linda joined the group. Diana got up, lifting their drinks and headed toward them. Wedging herself between Scott and Linda, she handed him one.

"This is for me, right?" Scott asked. He put his arm around her waist, and she doubted a soul in the group thought he meant the glass of wine.

Chapter 8

Decorated as a throwback to the art deco period, the hotel's ladies' lounge included private cornices where women could adjust their makeup under flattering lit mirrors. Diana sat in one of these at the end of the room. She'd checked her gown, which still sported perfect roses despite the heat her encounter had provoked.

Unknown to her, Linda Engles sat in one a few feet away.

"You won't believe what she looked like," Linda said to a woman Diana couldn't see.

"Has she gained a lot of weight?" the woman asked.

"It's not that. She's thin, but that rag of a dress she's wearing looks like she made it herself."

"Hmm," the other woman said. "I thought it was rather nice."

"Nice?" Linda questioned. "Could you imagine wearing that?"

"Are you kidding?" the woman said, her voice rising as if in surprised. "That dress is a Naeem Khan design, the same woman who designed a dress for Michelle Obama. Of course, I could imagine wearing it. I should be so lucky, but if Michael knew what that cost he'd divorce me."

"Well, she's no Michelle Obama."

"None of us are," the other woman said. "I better get back."

"I'll see you in a minute," Linda said as the door closed. "Designer, humph!" Linda said the word as if it tasted bad. Then she laughed, a high-pitched sound. It was the final straw. Diana had been trained in customer service. She knew how to defuse a situation, how to allow the customer to rant and rave until they were out of breath or had expended all the anger inside them. She'd spent years soothing nerves and offering alternatives, compromising angry patrons. She took all that knowledge, balled it in to a tight little wad and pitched it in the trash.

Approaching Linda, she walked right into her personal space. She knew what the reaction would be and Linda did not disappoint her. Sudden fear appeared on Scott's former girlfriend's face. She leaned away from Diana. Maybe she could feel the anger in the woman she'd teased for years, the one who was through with being the scapegoat or butt of jokes. Maybe Linda was or maybe she wasn't, but she was about to hear and see something she'd never seen before.

Diana kept her voice menacingly low even though the two of them had the room to themselves. Through clenched teeth she spoke, her lips barely moving. "I am not your whipping girl," she began. "I will no longer take your barbs or be the person on which you inflict darts. I am here with Scott Thomas at his invitation. If you don't like that, then I suggest you find your mink or sable or rat and get out of here. If you try this with me one more time, the secret you've been harboring for the last ten years will be spread all over Facebook and YouTube, as well as throughout Princeton and Rocky Hill. Then you'll know what it's like to be the butt of jokes. The lapdogs who crowd around you awaiting the favors you offer them will learn the truth about Linda Engles. See how quickly they abandon you and that phony smile you give them."

"What...what could you know?" She tried to act brave. "There is nothing to know."

Diana smiled at her, although the smile held more hostility than mirth. "I know it all. From the moment you entered that house on Michigan Avenue until you returned to your dorm. I know how many times you went there and what you did inside. And with whom?"

"How?" she asked.

"Does that matter? The point is I know."

Linda gasped. "Why...why wouldn't you have used this information before, *if* you have it?"

"Because, unlike you, I don't tell other people's secrets."

"But you're willing to divulge mine." Her voice was stronger.

"I've been pushed to the limit by you. I'm at the wall and there is no place else for me to go. If you think I'm going to let you grind me into the floor every time I see you, I want you to know that is not going to happen. You're done making fun of me and everyone else within my hearing. When you return to that room, you'll be the model of feminine hospitality. If you for one minute don't believe I'll make good on my promise, just try me."

Diana glared at her punctuating the point that this was no threat. It was a promise.

"I went there to volunteer," Linda stammered.

"Sure you did. You volunteered community service as part of your parole."

Linda's hand went to her breasts. Diana knew her heart was about to jump out of the strapless gown she wore.

Diana moved back, standing up straight. She kept her

gaze on Linda who'd gone as white as paste and looked as if a single breath could push her through the back wall.

"There has to be another reason," Linda said. "You wouldn't keep that information to yourself all these years to protect me. Not after the way I treated you." She stared at Diana for almost a minute. Then she sat up straight. The truth dawned on her. "You're in love with him," Linda stated.

Diana remained quiet, silenced as surely as if she had tape over her mouth.

"That's why you're doing this. Does he know?"

"I doubt it. And I doubt you're going to rush out of here and share the good news."

"What does my record have to do with Scott?"

"Don't you know? Can't you remember what he was back in school?"

Linda looked confused. "He was popular, outgoing, invited to all the parties. A big man on campus."

"All those things," Diana said. "He was a PolySci major. Political Science. Think about that."

"Yeah, so?" She opened her hands, questioning what one had to do with the other."

"He talked about law school, going into public office."

"That was all talk. None of us knew what we really wanted to do."

"Going to law school was a first step," Diana reminded her. "He even had application papers for the LSAT. I saw them."

"Scott has an uncle who's a lawyer. He worked in his office one summer and talked about going into that profession."

"And if he had, he'd be linked with you, a felon, a woman who had once served time for theft. What do you think his chances of getting elected would be then?"

"That's silly, no one would look at me. I wasn't married to him."

"But you wanted to be. You did everything in your power to get his ring on your finger. You'll have to tell me why that didn't work out someday."

Linda's face turned as red as it could under her over made up face and Diana's menacing countenance.

"My record is clean. No one could find a thing."

"*I* found it," Diana said. She straightened, stepped back and let the point sink in. "Have a wonderful evening." Diana walked to the door and left the room. Outside she stopped and inhaled a long breath. She'd never expected to let Linda know that she found out that she was seeing a parole officer during college. She came to Princeton a couple of years older than most freshmen. She told the story that she'd worked and decided to return to school because she understood that she wanted a career and not just a job. It sounded good coming from her, but what she'd really wanted was a husband.

She'd been caught shoplifting several times. She was convicted of theft and given parole and community service. She kept it quiet and far away from the old-money structures of Princeton proper. But Diana discovered her secret by accident. She'd been heading to New York to meet her sister when she saw Linda getting on the train. Why she followed her, Diana didn't know, but Diana got off the train and went to the house on Michigan. After that, Diana used her many skills as the geek Linda accused her of being and found out the rest.

Following her and finding out what was in that building was easy. Posing as a student doing research on the percentage of young felons who turn their lives around, she interviewed Linda's parole officer right after she left. With Linda's discussion still fresh in his mind, the parole officer gave Diana examples of young felons. While he didn't break any laws or infringe on any protocols, he cited the details. Diana filed the information away. Because Linda had been a minor, her record was expunged.

In a way Diana felt sorry for Linda. But tonight was the last time that Linda would walk on her. Diana was ready to battle anyone determined to wreck her relationship with Scott.

Scott smiled as Diana approached their table. He stood as if greeting her for the first time. Diana lifted her drink when she reached the table and drank before being reseated.

"Everything okay?" Scott asked.

"Everything is fine," she said, flashing him a brilliant smile. "Dance with me."

Together they went to the floor and she slipped into his arms as easily as anyone who knew her lover's every move. Diana felt great. She'd unleashed ten years of pent-up frustration, and the release was almost sexual.

"What happened in there?" Scott asked.

"In where?"

"Don't act you don't know what I'm taking about. I saw who went in first and who came out last. Did she—"

Diana shook her head. "Nothing happened. We talked. Everything is fine." And it was. Diana had only had a couple of glasses of wine, neither of which she finished. Yet she felt as if she were flying.

Scott leaned back and looked skeptically at her. "Are you sure?"

Diana's smile dazzled. She put her head next to his and danced. She wanted to close her eyes and fall into the music with him, but she remembered what happened at the Embry wedding and kept herself in check.

At the end of the night, the usual "let's keep in touch" messages and the exchanges of cell phone numbers and email addresses was done as the party broke up.

When they entered Diana's house minutes later, she was humming.

"You sound like you enjoyed the evening," Scott said.

"I did. It went much better than I thought it would."

"So you had reservations?" Scott asked.

"Didn't you?"

"Some," he admitted.

Diana sat down on the sofa and slipped her shoes off.

"It was amazing to see the look on everyone's faces when we walked in." Scott laughed.

Diana enjoyed hearing him laugh.

"And you were great when you defused that situation Linda started."

If only you knew. "It's my customer service training."

Scott moved to sit next to her. "Whatever it was," he said, "I was ready to change the dynamics of what was going on if need be. I didn't want this to turn into a night that humiliated you."

"I thank you for that," Diana told him. She propped her feet on the coffee table and stretched her legs out in front of her. Scott put his arm around her and she leaned against his shoulder. "You know," she began. "I *can* fight my own battles."

Silence followed her last statement. It stretched between them changing the friendly nature of the room to awkwardness. Scott stared at her. They were suddenly strangers, not knowing what to say or do next.

"Would you like something to drink?" Diana asked.

He shook his head, answering her silently. Then after another long moment, he stood up. "I think I'd better leave."

Diana was at a loss as to what to say. She didn't want him to go. Linda had read her right when she said Diana was in love with Scott. She was. They had made a deal to go to the dinner-dance together. It was a joke to begin with, but the last week had changed her. She thought it had changed him, too. Somewhere along the way, she'd begun to think their relationship was real, especially when he came to her aid in front of his friends and everyone else. The old Scott wouldn't have done that. The old Scott would be hand and fist in the corner with the Lindas of the world.

But this Scott wanted to kiss her. She knew it. The air between them sizzled with unfulfilled sex. Even when they danced, when he held her, she felt it, knew they wanted each other. But he was leaving. Diana felt as if the room got longer as he approached the door. But finally he had his hand on the knob. He was really going to leave. And she was going to let him. She didn't want to, but if she asked him to stay, everything would change. Diana wasn't ready for changes. She had her business to run and it was flourishing. She was involved in the community, sitting on several committees. She had friends, people who liked her for who she was. They didn't come with the baggage of her college years. They didn't know Brainiac or Diana 4.0. They accepted her for who she was now.

Scott opened the door and went through it. He pulled it shut. Diana heard the click of the lock. She went to the door to throw the deadbolt. The house was quiet, but she heard a rushing in her ears to rival the home team winning the Super Bowl.

Diana didn't understand how the door came to be open, but she was standing in it calling Scott's name. Her feet were bare, cold on the wooden porch. He stood next to his car, key in hand.

"Please stay," she said. Diana heard the words, recognized her voice, understood the implication of her request. And threw any caution her mind had left to the east wind.

Scott remained where he was. His body went still as he stared at her. Time seemed to stop its forward march as the two of them gazed at each other. Slowly he closed the car door and walked back to where she stood. Diana's mouth went dry. He was the sexiest man she'd ever seen. No longer was there any boyishness about him. Neither of them said a word when they were face to face. He cupped her face and stared in her eyes. Then let his eyes rove over her features until they settled on her mouth. Diana couldn't breathe. The noise in her head grew louder. He kissed her, tenderly, brushing his mouth over hers, teasing, tantalizing, promising more to come. Her arms wrapped around him and she pulled him close.

Scott pushed her backward and kicked the door closed. Reaching behind him, he secured the deadbolt without once lifting his mouth from hers. Diana felt his length pressing against her. His arousal was unmistakable. She moved against it, and he groaned in her mouth, a sound so guttural and pleasurable it sent prickles up her arms. Scott's hands caressed her back, making long, slow sweeps over the fabric of her dress. She could have been wearing a sheer nightgown. She could feel the heat of his hands all the way to her skin.

When his hands smoothed over her bottom, a wave of pleasure slammed into her, pushing her further into him. She heard the rasp of the dress zipper as he pulled it down. Cool air replaced the heat building inside her. When he reached the base of the dress, his hand slipped inside. Diana's head fell back. Her body was suffused with a red-hot fire that had her crying out. Scott pushed it away from her. A royal-blue puddle formed at her feet.

Wearing only a bra and panties, Diana bit her lip to

hold in all waves of rapture vying for an outlet. This was the climax of her life to this point. She'd always wanted Scott. From that first encounter on campus to this moment, she wanted him to make love to her. She wanted to be in his arms, wanted to hold him and have him hold her. She wanted his mouth of her body and wanted his skin on her skin.

Scott must have pulled his tie loose after he left her front door. Diana caught one of the ends and slipped it free of his neck. She held it out the length of her arm and dropped it to the floor. Then her fingers worked the buttons of his dress shirt. As she released one button, her head bent and she pressed her mouth to him. His skin was moist as her sure fingers spread over him. Together they undressed each other, leaving a trail of clothes as they circled each other on the way to her bedroom.

The room was lit only by the moonlight. Scott released her bra and it fell to the floor. His thumbs brushed over her nipples, which grew to hard peaks under his tutelage. Diana clung to him. Her knees were weak, and with what he was doing to her, she wasn't going to be able to support herself much longer. They divested themselves of their final garments, and her heated skin met a torrent of fire. Scott turned Diana around and pulled her back into his front. His hands traveled all over her then settled over her breasts, and he brought her body to life as he gently massaged them.

The gentle pleasure Scott evoked in her as his hands moved over her, stopping and starting in places she never knew could add to her pleasure, built until she was panting and turning in his arms. Her body was hot and ready. She could feel herself flowing, wanting to be satisfied. Her inner muscles tightened to the point that she had to have him.

Together they fell on the bed. Scott quickly grabbed a condom, then he protected them and in one swift movement they joined. His mouth found her and he began the timeless rhythm of love. She opened her legs, allowing him greater access and wallowing in the pleasure that went through her with each pull and push of their bodies. His hands reached around to clasp her bottom. He lifted her to him, stroking harder and harder, increasing the pleasure quotient. Diana heard the sounds around them. She was unsure if they were from her or from him, but with each joining of their bodies the rhythm grew. They worked harder and faster. Her heart beat out of control. Her hands and arms held him, moved over him, pulled him into her, filling her with the love she always knew would be there.

Together they headed for oblivion, for the climax that came like a crashing wave. The roar started low, then stepped up one stair at a time until it reached the zenith of intensity, until it was impossible to do anything other than explode.

And explode they did.

The coffee cup on Scott's desk had the Edward's Coffee Shop logo on it. He lifted it and looked at the black writing on white paper. It reminded him of Diana. During the past couple of weeks it seemed everything reminded him of her. And it was all good. He laughed to himself. Some of it was fun. Not like the fun he had when he was a sophomoric prankster. He didn't want to make fun of her. He wanted to have fun *with* her. Last night had created a memory he could hold and bring out when he needed to think of something good. It was their dance together. Despite his buddies' comments, he enjoyed holding her close, and he wasn't even sorry that they had seen him dancing with her as if she was the only woman for him.

He wasn't sorry when they made love, either. He wanted to stay with her to repeat the all-consuming act again and again. But eventually they had to eat, and both had to work. This was what Scott should have been doing now, instead of reliving their wild night on the sheets.

The door opened, and in walked three burly men. Scott sat up straight in his chair. He recognized them, had been expecting them in some form: a phone call, email, text. But they were here in person.

They were his friends, had been since college. And each one knew him and how they all treated Diana. When he was not flying a corporate executive to a meeting or going up to Maine, they got together for a guys' night out. They'd drink and talk about their wives, sometimes about the women who got away, and invariably come around to Scott's state of singleness. Someone would always ask if he'd met anyone special, when was he going to settle down or mention someone they'd known in their collective pasts who was now divorced. Women would be surprised to know that men tried just as hard to introduce their single male friends to women as they did.

Dan's and Mike's wives were willing to introduce him to one of their friends. Scott declined every time. From what he heard them saying, marriage was great, but there were times when it was trying. So far he hadn't met anyone he wanted to spend his life with.

Scott set the paper cup down and leaned back in his chair, linking his fingers together and placing his hands on his abdomen. The guys approached him seemingly in slow motion, like the astronauts in *The Right Stuff*. And undoubtedly, he was about to be told the right stuff.

"You're late," Scott said, getting in the first strike. "I expected you to show up for breakfast."

When they met, they always had beer. Today, Hunt set a

bag of sandwiches on the desk along with mega-size cups containing soft drinks. Without a word they dove in and pulled out food. Scott didn't reach for the bag, but Hunt slid a wrapped sandwich and a cup toward him.

"What's going on?" Mike asked. He spun a chair around and straddled it. Dan lowered his bulk into the worn leather chair of questionable origin. And Huntley Christenson, called Hunt by everyone who knew him, pulled a rolling office chair from a nearby desk. They looked like the dissertation committee except for the food.

"I'm sorry I missed the party," Hunt said. "Sounds like you and Diana 4.0 were the highlight of the evening."

"Don't call her that," Scott snapped. He came forward in the chair. Three pairs of eyes stared at him.

"Scott are you serious about her?" Dan asked.

"No," he said quickly. The truth was he didn't know how he felt about Diana. He did have feelings for her, more than even he was willing to admit.

"What was the dance about then?" Dan asked. "You showing up with her was bound to spark rumors."

Scott smiled. He thought of them sitting in the arch and planning this. "At first it was a joke," he said. He explained about them seeing the irony of a date together, especially one that would take them in direct view of the same people they went to school with.

"So you two came as a joke?"

"It started out that way."

"Okay," Hunt said. "Why don't you start at the beginning and tell us what's going on?"

"And I would do this why?" Scott asked. "You're my friends, not my parents."

"It's damn interesting," Dan said. "And Diana 4.0 is the last person we'd ever pair with you."

"Don't call her that," he said again. "That was a college

thing and a poor one at that. We should all have had 4.0 averages. She's a professional now with her own business."

Silence spread over the small group.

"This is your fault," Scott said, looking at them.

"How's that?" Mike asked.

"It started at your wedding."

"Mine? I've only been married a few months. Don't you mean Bill's wedding?"

"You weren't there," Scott told Mike. "You were off on your honeymoon. After the reception, we were all sitting around. The usual began and as usual conversation rolled around to my love life."

"Or lack thereof," Hunt interjected.

"We always do that," Dan defended. "It's all in fun. We don't mean anything by it."

"Just because we always do it doesn't mean we should," Scott told them. "Like we shouldn't continue to think of Diana in the negative because of her brain."

"This coming from the leader of the pack."

Scott nodded. "I admit it. I did taunt her when we were in school, but we're in our thirties now. We have jobs, responsibilities, you have wives. Would you want someone from their pasts referring to your wives with negative comments?"

They sobered and looked at each other.

"You're really stuck on her," Hunt said. "When did this happen?"

Scott took a moment to collect his thoughts. "After Mike's wedding, you guys really laid it on heavy."

They hung their heads a moment then nodded.

"It stayed on my mind, and one night while I was on-line one of those ads for singles popped up. I don't even remember clicking on it, but when the window opened I had no intention of doing anything but reading. Then I saw the questions and I started answering them, entering information."

"And you got Diana—" Mike stopped himself from adding the *4.0* to the end of Diana's name.

Scott nodded, keeping the rest of what he'd entered to himself. "I didn't know it was her for months. We didn't include photos and we never used real names. It wasn't until we met in person that we discovered we knew each other."

"And you started dating."

Scott shook his head. "We had one dinner, but I was called away. The scholarship dinner-dance was the first time we went anywhere together."

"Are you going out again?" Dan asked.

"We have no plans, but I'm thinking of it," he answered honestly. "She's different from how we perceived her in school."

"What about Linda?" Hunt asked. "I hear she's back and gunning for you."

"Not interested," Scott said. "She's not much different from when we were in school. I suppose we all don't change."

"Maybe she *is* changing, too," Mike said.

Scott looked at him for an additional explanation.

"At first she was as mean to Diana as she always was. But later in the evening I heard her give Diana a compliment."

"What did she say?" Scott asked. He'd witnessed Linda's treatment of Diana. But after Diana returned from the ladies' lounge something was different.

"She liked her dress and her hair," Mike said.

Scott remembered the royal-blue dress Diana wore and the way her hair was. She'd done it in a huge, thick collection of curls that dangled down her back. He also remembered removing the dress and undoing her hair. After that he was the one who was undone.

"Are you sure that was a compliment?" Scott asked.

"She didn't sound as if it was tipped with her usual venom. In fact, I was surprised to hear her speak without the sarcasm that usually poured from her lips."

Scott remembered the comment from across the years. Diana wasn't the only person they ridiculed. Linda got her share of colorful remarks from the group, some in private, some to her face.

"If Linda complimented Diana," Scott said, "she wants something."

"Or she's planning something," Hunt added. His tone had them looking at him.

"Do you know something about Linda?"

"Not about her and Diana, but I know what she wants."

"How?" Dan asked. "You weren't at the dance."

Hunt said nothing, only stared back at Scott.

"Well, don't keep us in suspense," Dan finally said.

"What's she's always wanted—you," he said quietly.

All eyes turned to Scott.

Chapter 9

Scott set the plane down and rushed to complete the post-flight paperwork. He was meeting Diana and that was uppermost in his mind. He knew he couldn't skimp on what was necessary with the plane, but he was glad to be able to turn it over to the mechanics and take a quick shower before heading into town.

They had no formal plans, just dinner and relaxing at his place.

Teddy was leaving as he arrived. "Hello, Scott. Good night, Scott," she called with a wave as she headed toward her car. The parking lot was crowded with construction material. The men had ended their work for the day. Scott had to step around cement bags and discarded wood and broken pieces of drywall to reach the door.

He brushed away a sheen of dust before climbing the stairs to Diana's office. She met him at the door, and all thoughts went to her. Kissing her on the mouth, he stepped back and surveyed her.

"You look like you had a successful day."

"I did. I only have a few details to complete and another Weddings by Diana will be up and running.

"Congratulations. We'll have to celebrate. But let's not do it here. There is so much debris outside."

"Where did you go today?" Diana asked when they were in his Lexus and heading away from the parking lot.

"Tennessee."

She laughed. "That sounds so interesting. Most people would answer 'nowhere' or 'out to lunch.' You get to visit entire states."

"Today I didn't get to see much of it. I only thought of getting back to you."

"Ooooh, pretty words. I love hearing them."

The drive was short. Scott led her to one of the older neighborhoods outside Princeton proper. While both the borough and the main section of town referred to as Princeton proper had merged, it would take a while before the sense of separation ended. Scott lived on one of the side streets close to the gothic-looking high school.

They got out of the car and he carried in several bags.

"What are we eating?" Diana asked.

"Wine and cheese."

"Is that all? I think I'm starving tonight."

"There might be a steak in one of these."

"Red meat. Suppose I don't eat red meat?"

"I've already seen you eat it."

He put the bags on the kitchen counter and started to remove the items. Diana looked around the room. His kitchen wasn't state-of-the-art like hers, but it was functional and easy to get around in. She moved through and looked into the living room.

"The light switch is on the right," Scott said. Diana found it and turned it on. The room had the basic furniture and artifacts he'd brought back from his travels.

"This is beautiful," she said and stepped into the room.

Scott went to the doorway and watched her. She stared at a painting over the fireplace.

"It's the Maine house," he explained. "We used to go there often. I learned to fly there. Ever been?"

Diana shook her head. Scott handed her a glass of sparkling wine and told her it was her turn to make the salad. She rejoined him in the kitchen and opened several drawers looking for the silverware. The kitchen quickly filled with savory smells. Once dinner was ready, they sat down in his kitchen and ate.

"I had a very interesting meeting last week," he said. He didn't know why he wanted to tell her about it, but he wanted her to know.

"Really?" she said, smiling as she sipped wine. "Was it about me?"

"As self-centered as ever," he teased, using the same phrase she had when he'd asked the same question. She laughed, and he loved hearing the tinkle in her voice.

"The meeting was no laughing matter. It was almost an intervention."

"Intervention?"

They got up and moved from the kitchen to the living room. "And your name did come up."

"This doesn't sound good."

Scott related what had happened, casting a good light on it.

"So they've changed and no longer think of me as Diana 4.0?"

"That might take some time," he admitted. "But being a 4.0 student is a compliment."

"Not the way they said it. But I suppose since you've changed your thinking, I can at least give them the benefit of the doubt until proven otherwise."

"You say that as if you expect them to prove otherwise."

"Well, there is Princeton borough and Princeton proper. And never the twain shall meet."

"They'll come around when they get to know you."

Scott realized he wanted them to get to know her. He wanted them to realize how they had misjudged her when they were in school, but now that they were older, more mature, they could see her for the warm, loving person she was.

"What are we going to do tonight?" she asked, apparently relegating his friends to another subject area. "We could go for a walk."

Scott stood up. "I have a better idea, but it does involve a walk."

Diana looked at Scott and a slow smile teased his mouth. He came to her. Diana didn't turn away. She was no longer Diana 4.0 or Brainiac. She was a woman, and Scott was the man attracted to her. His hands were on her waist, the same as they had been at the Embry wedding rehearsal.

"Shouldn't we clean the dishes?" she suggested, her voice a low whisper.

"What dishes?" he asked.

She looked in his eyes, seeing the need there. His mouth slid down to hers. The moment their lips touched, Diana was transported back to school on *that* day, back to the kissing spot. Scott's arms went around her, pulling her close to him. He tilted his head took her full mouth. His tongue swept inside and she joined him, weaving her arms around his neck and feeling the warm softness of smooth skin.

Without her high heels, Diana felt short next to Scott. Pushing herself up on her toes, she leaned into him, wrapping one leg around Scott's. The action brought her body closer to his. She could feel his erection grow hard against her belly. A low, pleasurable sound came from him. The feeling was too good for her to stop. She didn't want to think about anything but him. Scott's hand caressed her back, traveling up and down over her contours.

His hands warmed her where they touched. And he touched her everywhere. Each part of her shirt and the tops of her pants turned to fire as Scott skimmed over them. Diana was sure her skin would burn and slide off. Her second leg raised as she could think only of getting closer to him. Scott grasped her bottom and held her, pushing into her. The two became one.

"Where's the bedroom?" she asked in a croaky voice.

"Top of the stairs."

Diana didn't know how they made it. It seemed to take hours to get there. Scott stopped along the steps, pushing her back into the rungs and deepening the kiss with each lift of his head. His fingers slid between hers and they stretched along the stairs. She could only marvel that they kept themselves from sliding down the stairs. By the time they got to the bed, both were frenzied. They tore at their clothes and undressed each other, separating and coming together as if each needed the other to survive.

Scott pulled Diana back to him and kissed her. Each stood naked in the other's arms. Diana inhaled Scott's scent. She smelled his flight jacket combined with the outdoors. His body was hard and smooth. Her hands ran over him as if he were clay and she was the artist forming him into a man. His butt was strong, and she reveled over the curves leading to his long legs. Her fingers forced him to arch into her.

The whole room smelled of sexual electricity, combined with the guttural stock of human pleasure. Scott laid her on the bed and joined her there. His eyes gazed over her, taking in the smooth skin of her breasts and legs. He kissed her neck, then her cheeks, neck and shoulders. As he neared her breasts, Diana could feel them grow heavy and point upward in anticipation. She was having trouble controlling her breathing.

Scott paused at her navel, giving it wet attention. Diana writhed beneath him. She wanted him now, but he wasn't finished with his torture. His hands stretched down the outside of her legs and came up the inside. When he reached the juncture of her legs, he used his thumb to give attention to the sweet spot of her sex.

"Awww," she cried out. Her hands took his shoulders and assisted him up to her. She opened her legs in invitation, and Scott protected himself before entering her. Diana's eyes fluttered shut as she moved ever so slightly. Yet the pleasure he evoked shot through her like a narcotic, instantly taking her on a high greater than she'd ever felt before. Three, four, five times the rapture embraced them. Waves burned inside her. Her fingers grabbed his back and held him, guided him, showing him where her pleasure points were and having him tap into each of them.

With each thrust of his legs, Diana was sure she would die. Yet each was greater, harder, more intense, more sensitive and found a higher level of pleasure than the one before. Unsure if she could endure this plane of erotic saturation, she still didn't want him to stop. She anticipated each thrust, waited for it, wanted it, wanted more and more, wanted it all.

She heard Scott's sounds as he pushed into her. Her head banged against the bed's headboard. Diana pushed against it, stretching her body and allowing him greater access to the core of her being. It could have gone on for years or been over in a few seconds, she didn't know. Time had no place in their lovemaking. Only feelings counted. Only the area of space where they ascended—where the universe was composed of sensation, where the giving and receiving of pleasure was the purpose of life—existed. And only the two of them inhabited it.

The break happened, the big bang, the eruption of a shattering star penetrated her mind. Diana felt the wind of creation rush over her. She heard the scream, yet didn't know it came from her. When they could get no higher, feel no greater pleasure in each other, they came, climaxed, in the bright light of their new world.

Seven nights, Diana thought. Seven glorious love-filled nights. She glanced from the mirror to the hotel bed. She would miss him tonight. Scott had been with her every night, and they'd burned up the sheets with their lovemaking. Diana whirled before the mirror. She wore a business suit, but she felt beautiful.

The opening of the latest franchise was days away, and she'd flown to Montana for some last-minute details. Several calls to Scott proved fruitless. She missed him every time. She assumed he had an emergency and had to fly out quickly. But he was never far from her thoughts or from the infusion of heat that accompanied those thoughts.

Going to the new office, Diana worked with Carrie Osgood, its manager. They spent hours together and by the end of the day the room was cluttered with material: glossy magazines, wedding veils, blueprints and flowers. Coffee cups and the debris of a working lunch lay on the credenza in the corner.

"Many of the details have been worked out. I've been arranging for furniture and inventory. The suppliers you use have been wonderful to work with, and several orders are in the works. I made a contact with a local office supply company, and our furniture arrives tomorrow."

Diana listened as Carrie updated her on the franchise's progress since Diana's last visit.

"Are we still on for the grand opening?" Diana asked.

"We'll be ready," she said without hesitation. "The shelves are all in place. Our inventory will be here in a few days." Carrie spread her arms and Diana looked at the empty shelves, glass cases, mirrors and dressing rooms. Carrie's idea was that the franchise should have a working bridal shop in case brides wanted a one-stop for all wedding consultants. Diana loved the idea. And it was another place to showcase Teddy's designs.

"I've worked with the advertising firm I used in the past," Diana told her. "They've begun the program. A reception and fashion show to introduce the business usually works well to bring in potential clients." Diana held her hands out with her fingers crossed. "It will work again."

"I already have a client," Carrie said.

"Is it a friend?" Diana asked. That was the usual way planners began.

"Not a friend. It was a recommendation. She's not the richest person. She took the basic package."

"No matter the package, treat her like royalty. This is her day. If she likes what she gets, she'll tell her friends, and our business lives or dies on word of mouth."

Diana gathered her papers and briefcase. Sliding her purse on her shoulder, she smiled at Carrie. "You'll do fine," Diana told her confidently. "And you won't be alone. We'll have one of our best consultants come out and help you until you can hire someone of your own."

Carrie took a breath. Diana smiled and squeezed her shoulder. "I'm off to the airport. Just follow the details we set out in the package and everything will work out fine."

Carrie nodded, but Diana understood she wasn't taking to being alone for the first time. She'd be fine. Mistakes could happen, but usually they were fixable. And Diana had a full team of people who came as backup.

She only wished she had the same kind of team for her life. Things were going well—too well—and that scared her.

Diana was both tired and exhilarated when she returned to the hotel that night. Her plans were to order room service, take a hot shower and turn in early. She'd fly home in the morning and straight into Scott's arms if he was back.

She called him as soon as she got to the room. He answered, and her heartbeat accelerated just hearing his voice.

"Where are you?" she asked, expecting to hear he was in New York or Timbuktu.

"Montana," he said.

Diana was sure she hadn't heard him correctly. She moved her hair and pushed the phone closer to her ear. "Where?"

"Outside your door," he said.

Diana was robbed of the ability to speak. She tried saying something, but nothing came out. She turned and stared at the closed door. She was sure she hadn't heard correctly. It had to be the phone. She was due for a new one. This was the time to get it.

"Open the door," he said.

Obediently, she went to the hotel door and peered through the fisheye lens. Scott stood there in his flight suit. Yanking the door inward, she found it was true.

"What are you doing here?"

He didn't answer. He swept into the room and took her into his arms. They kissed for a long time.

"I couldn't wait one more day for you to come back," he said, kissing her again.

Diana couldn't get a word in, and after a moment she didn't want to. Feelings took over her body, and she only wanted to know Scott's hands on her, feel him filling her with more pleasure than should be legal.

Diana opened her eyes and groaned at the sound of Scott's ringing phone. Reaching across her, he grabbed it from the bedside table.

"Hello," he said. Then, like a soldier coming to attention, he was instantly alert. He got out of bed, listening intently.

"Linda," he said. "What?"

He waited for her to answer.

"Where?" After another pause, he said, "I'm on my way."

Scott ended the call and grabbed his clothes. Looking around for his socks, he suddenly remembered Diana. She lay in bed, her body raised on her elbows, the sheet covering her naked breasts.

"I have to go," he said. Going into the bathroom, he showered and dressed in ten minutes. Taking a second, he kissed her quickly and left the hotel room. It was unusual for him to get a job outside his usual flying area, but he'd been called to pick up a sick child in need of emergency microsurgery. Scott understood the crucial nature of his job. He was at the airport and onto his plane in record time. Soaring through the air, it suddenly hit him. What he'd said. What Diana had heard. And the worst of it was the dispatcher's name was Linda. She probably thought he was rushing off to meet his former girlfriend Linda.

Nothing could be further from the truth. Scott need to call Diana. Explain. Let her know where he was and who had called to give him the message. Anything he'd say in the cockpit would be recorded on the black box that had been placed there for security purposes in case of an accident. There was an air phone in the cockpit, another FAA safety feature in case communication was interrupted by other sources.

He grabbed it and dialed. No answer.

Slamming the phone back into its cradle, he mentally kicked himself. He remembered her lying under the sheets. Her hair was all around her, but the expression on her face had been questioning. He had seen it, but didn't think too much of it. His mind was on the life he had to save. But Diana didn't know that was his destination. He was sure she only heard the word *Linda*. It was Linda Tisdale, the dispatcher for the medical air facility. Not Linda Engles, his former girlfriend. But Diana didn't know there were two different Lindas.

Even after last night, after the passionate and uncontrollable fervor of their lovemaking, the pure consummation of the universe, she would think it was all a lie, that he'd left her bed only to jump into one with his former girlfriend. He needed to talk to Diana, but there was no way. He had an injured child on board and every minute counted in getting that child medical care.

Scott would have to explain later. He'd come to Montana to explain that he loved her. Yet he'd never said the words. He'd shown her in every way possible, but the three little words remained in his mind and his heart. On the outside, the side she could see and hear, his actions said he was leaving her.

He checked the controls. Everything was in order. His life was a mess, but the plane was flying as he had programmed it to. Every second it took him farther and farther away from the woman he loved. She was probably on her way traveling east. He was flying to Los Angeles. The child behind the closed door of the aircraft was a six-year-old brain-tumor patient on her way for microsurgery at the world-renowned Oceanic Clinic. When Scott had got to the airport, the ambulance was already there and she, along with a truckload of medical equipment, was on board.

The tower cleared him immediately and then they were airborne. He was winging his way four thousand miles from where Diana was headed. He could only hope when he got to the ground she would answer the phone and allow him to explain.

But that wasn't going to happen. Scott wasn't allowed to take off immediately and return to his home base. He'd been in the air too long within the last twenty-four hours. He had to stay where he was for at least another night. Diana not answering his calls told him she believed he was with Linda Engles. No matter how many messages he left, she returned none of them.

Packing wasn't one of the things Diana did well. Even though she traveled a lot, she'd never learned to pack her clothes efficiently. After Scott left, she cared nothing about packing. She virtually threw her clothes into her suitcase and smashed it shut. If the people at the airline wanted to open and inspect it, so be it. She didn't care if they found her dirty nightgown and underwear.

How could Scott just jump up and leave without a single word? And how could he go to Linda? He'd told her Linda was old news. That she was not coming back into his life, yet one call from her when he was two thousand miles away and he'd grabbed his clothes and left Diana's bed.

She'd never felt so abandoned. Diana hated to admit it, but Scott still had feelings for Linda. Diana couldn't compete with that. She'd already known they'd had no future together, but he'd treated her well, made her feel special.

But she only had a few months with him, and he and Linda had years of time that linked them together.

"Checking out," she told the woman at the hotel desk and then settled her bill.

"I hope you enjoyed your stay and you'll come back again."

Diana returned the young woman's smile, although she felt more like crying than smiling. She never wanted to see this place again. The best and worst day of her life had been spent here. Scott had made love to her so sweetly and so tenderly that she felt as if nothing on earth could top it. She'd thought of happily-ever-after, of being the bride in her own wedding. And then the worst had happened.

He'd left her.

Alone.

And without a word.

Princeton, New Jersey, was as much a tourist attraction as the Statue of Liberty. Droves of people flocked to see the university. Scott was among the many locals walking along the short stretch of land that comprised the center of town. He hoped to see Diana going into the coffee shop. He'd been back a day and she hadn't answered her phone or returned any of his messages.

She loved Edward's coffee. Scott figured he'd run into her here sooner or later. Going through the door, he looked around, but she wasn't among the patrons. He ordered a coffee and sat on one of the high chairs near the window that faced the university. If she came in he could talk to her. If she passed by he could go out and meet her.

"Is this seat taken?" someone asked.

"No." Scott turned and spoke at the same time. Slipping into the empty chair next to him was Linda, the last person he wanted to see. And the one person he didn't want Diana to find him with.

"I was hoping to run into you." Her voice was as soft as purring kitten.

"Why is that?" Scott wanted to leave. His strategy for the day had been thwarted. He couldn't leave now that she'd begun a conversation.

"Well, I'm back in town, and since I haven't been here for a while, I thought we might get together for old time's sake. You could tell me what's happening with the old crowd and we can catch up on each other's lives."

"You know this is a small town, but I was never the one who had that information. You should contact one of the women you used to hang out with. A couple of them are still around. At least they were at the dinner. I'm out of town a lot."

"I know, but they don't…" She moved closer to him.

Scott recognized the move. He and Linda had once been a couple. He didn't know what he'd seen in her.

"Linda," Scott began before she could go on. "We spent a lot of time together in the past."

"Yes," she smiled.

"Both of us have changed since then. You've been married and divorced. You're putting down roots in Rocky Hill."

"And you've flown all over the world. We could—"

"No," Scott stopped her. "We had—"

"I was only going to say that we had a great time at the dance, but don't read anything into it."

Scott understood she knew where he was going and had interrupted him to save face.

"Like you say, I've just moved back to the area. And I need to give myself some time since the divorce before I rush into anything." She laughed. He knew she was attempting to lighten the mood, but it failed. "I wouldn't want to make another mistake like the last one."

"Taking time to think things through is always a good decision."

She gave him a brilliant smile. "There is one thing I want to say."

"What's that?"

"Thank you."

Scott frowned. "For what?"

"For being my friend. I don't have many. I hope in the future I can continue to count you among them.'

"You can."

She leaned forward and kissed him on the cheek. At that exact moment, Diana's car stopped across the street to wait for the light. She looked directly at him, holding her gaze for a long moment.

"Damn," he cursed. Could things get any worse?

"Anything wrong?" Linda asked. Her gaze went to the Porsche.

The light turned green and Diana drove away.

Scott had no doubt that she'd recognized Linda.

"Is she the one?" Linda asked.

Scott barely heard the question. He continued to stare through the glass, looking at the space where Diana had witnessed an innocent kiss, a friendship kiss, between him and a former girlfriend. He knew Linda could be a conniving individual, but he didn't think she was insincere.

"I have to go," he said.

He left the cup on the counter and moved toward the door.

"Scott," Linda called.

He looked back at her.

"Tell her," she said.

Chapter 10

Diana knew she was acting like an idiot, but she didn't care. It was childish not to answer a phone or respond to a text message. She could tell Scott she didn't want to talk to him or she could listen to his explanation. Instead she'd taken the coward's way out and just refused to confront the fear that he might want to be with Linda Engles and not with her.

Diana had never called him and asked him to drop everything and come to her. She wondered it he would. Even if he was halfway across the country, would he fly to her the way he'd flown to Linda? She wasn't sure. She'd never tested anything and had no will to do so now. She didn't have the same history with him that Linda had. He and Linda had been lovers for three years. Diana barely had three months. But she thought the degree of intensity of their lovemaking made up for the shortness of time. It had for her.

When she thought about it, she and Scott didn't know each other that well. They knew the basics, like what it was like to make love, where they could touch each other to send their bodies into overdrive, but the mundane things—like what it was like growing up, when was his birthday, what was his favorite color—were things they hadn't been together long enough to learn. And now it was likely they never would.

Diana got out of the car feeling like stamping her feet. Instead, she slammed the car door, deciding it was time to chart her own life—without Scott. He preferred women like Linda. Diana would never be like her. And she'd make sure Scott didn't figure into her plans. She knew the Lindas of the world, and if he wanted to spend his time or his life with someone of her character, he had her permission.

And good riddance.

Diana entered the church. Seeing Scott and Linda in the window kissing had sent her nerves into burning jealousy. She hated to admit it to herself, but she wanted Scott and didn't like knowing he preferred Linda.

The quiet solitude of the sanctuary calmed her. She was backing Teddy up, but her partner was in control. Diana breathed slowly, allowing her heart to return to a normal beat, and smiled as the procession began.

Her cell phone vibrated as the bride and groom joined hands. Slipping outside, Diana pulled the phone free and checked the display. Suddenly she went cold. On the small display was his MatchforLove.com email address. She hadn't answered any of his calls. The message was a text. Diana stared at the small screen, unable to speak. She'd stopped listening to his messages. The sound of his voice sent her body into overdrive. She wanted to talk to him, but she wouldn't, couldn't. She couldn't trust herself not to forgive him of everything just because that deep voice had whispered in her ear and driven her crazy with desire.

Staring at the phone, she tried to decide if she should answer it. Should she open it and see what he had to say? Her finger was on the delete key. All she had to do was press it and the message would be gone. Her nerves would remain intact and she could return to the wedding. Finally, she opened the email. It said, *Call Emergency Health Flight Services—NOW!* The capital letters jumped off the screen. What happened? Why would she need to call Emergency Health Services? Scott worked there, but she knew no one there, had no dealings with anyone except Scott who even knew of the service.

A phone number accompanied the message, but it didn't specify anyone in particular to ask for. The message was from Scott's email address. Not a personal address, but the one he used for MatchforLove.com. Suddenly Diana panicked. Had anything happened to him? She leaned against the garden wall, her legs suddenly weak, her breath caught in her throat. She'd just seen him. The two of them.

It could be a ruse, but Diana couldn't take the chance. Maybe something had happened to Scott and he needed to reach her. She had to answer. She needed to know. If the message was from him, she could ignore it if she chose.

Immediately, she dialed the number. A woman answered. "This is Diana Greer. I have a message to call this number. Is anything wrong?"

"You need to come here right away," the woman said.

"Why? What's wrong?"

"Do you know where we are?"

Diana knew. There was only one airfield in the Princeton area, and Emergency Health Flight Services had their office and planes there.

"Please get here as soon as possible."

"Has something happened to Scott?" Diana's heart was pounding so hard, she could barely hear. Her grip on the small instrument was tight enough to crush it. Her voice grew louder as she tried to get some information.

"I have to go," she said. "We have another emergency."

The woman on the phone would give her no other information, only that it involved Scott. Diana stopped. She slowed her breathing. She had not said that Scott was the emergency. She hadn't said he wasn't, either.

Diana stepped back inside and signaled Teddy. Then she dialed Scott's number. No answer. She called his landline. Again no answer. Diana had to get there. She gave Teddy a shortened version of what occurred and told her she was leaving. Teddy assured her everything was under control.

Diana rushed to the car and sped through the zigzag streets of the township. Route 206 was only a one-lane road, and traffic stopped and started oblivious of her need to open the engine and run every stoplight to get to Scott. Finally she turned into the long driveway and sped down it. She parked in the first available space, not taking into account whether the space was legal or not.

Diana yanked open the door to a cavernous building, then entered and found a long wooden desk with a fifty-something woman behind it.

"Hello, I'm Diana Greer. I talked to someone on the phone."

"That was me," the woman said. "Catherine Manfred." She offered her hand. Diana shook it.

"Is Scott all right? Has he been hurt?" Diana didn't recognize her own voice. She'd rushed from the wedding and could account for the out-of-breath sound, but the catch in her throat was unexpected.

Instead of answering, Catherine Manfred handed Diana a folder. Diana opened it and found a report showing flight information from Montana to Los Angeles and a medical condition.

"Scott had a heart attack?" Diana could hardly speak. Each word came out separately. Her legs went numb and she gripped the counter, unsure if she could remain standing. "Where is he?"

"Hold on," Catherine said. She rushed around the counter and supported Diana around the waist, leading her to a chair where she sat.

"I'm sorry I frightened you. Scott is not here."

"Where is he?"

"He went to get something to eat, but I saw him go into the hangar a few moments ago."

"But he texted me," Diana said. "Said there was an emergency and I needed to come."

"Sorry, that was me. Scott was headed out. While he checked on something with the plane, I snagged his cell phone and left you the message. I needed to talk to you."

"Why?" Diana asked, looking at the stranger with wide eyes.

"Because you need to talk to him. He's a changed man since you stopped taking his calls. He's irritable and angry and hard to get along with."

"That may not be because of me."

"Believe me," Catherine said, "it's because of you."

Somehow that made Diana feel better. She was glad to hear that he was having at least as much misery as she was.

"If Scott didn't have a heart attack, why did you give me this?" She indicated the folder in her hand.

"It doesn't say anyone had a heart attack. We're not privy to medical details."

Diana looked inside again. She didn't understand what Catherine was trying to say.

"That's why he left you in Montana," she said. Diana looked up. The woman obviously knew more than Diana thought she should, but Diana was still confused.

"If you look closer, you'll see that he piloted a flight

where he picked up a child in Waymon Valley, Montana, and flew out to Los Angeles on the day he left you."

Diana checked the dates. She was aware of the exact date and time he'd left her.

"Because of him the lives of hundreds of children have been saved, including the one he brought to New York several days ago. It was all over the news."

Diana remembered the story. "But the call was from Linda."

"And you assumed it was Linda Engles, the vamp who's been calling here for days trying to get Scott to give her some attention."

"I didn't know that."

"Linda Tisdale is a scheduling and dispatch coordinator who works here. *She* called Scott that day. He was in Montana and convenient for getting the child to L.A. on time. Scott let us know he was going to Montana. Of course, he hadn't told us about you at the time and we didn't ask. When we got the call relayed from another emergency service that couldn't respond, he was in a perfect location. As you could tell, he didn't hesitate to answer."

"I feel like such an idiot. I wouldn't talk to him, wouldn't let him explain."

"All is not lost," Catherine said. Her tone was that of a loving mother. "You have a chance to say you're sorry."

"Thank you," Diana said.

"There's just one thing I want you to do."

Diana nodded.

"Don't tell Scott I interfered. He hates that."

Diana laughed.

"You know how men like to think they can handle their own problems," the woman said.

"Women, too."

* * *

When Diana misjudged someone, she did it on a grand scale. She left the Emergency Health Flight Servies offices, her feet dragging as if she were trying to carry a weight three times her size. How could she have been so wrong? And how could Scott let her believe that he was going to see Linda when all along he was rushing away to save someone's life? She'd told him once he was one of the good guys, yet she didn't let that knowledge keep her from destroying his character when it came to Linda Engles.

Right now Diana needed to talk to Scott. She needed to apologize for her comments, for what she thought of him. She pulled her cell out and dialed his number. She got his voice mail. Disconnecting without leaving a message, she wondered if he was ignoring her calls, since she'd ignored his. She wondered where he was. Where could she find him?

She started into a fast walk, then ran toward the hangar where Scott kept the corporate jet he flew. The wind pulled the curl out of her hair. By the time she reached the edge of the building she was out of breath. The shaded interior temporarily blinded her. It took a moment for her eyes to adjust from the bright sunshine outside.

"Scott," she called. Her voice was weak, and in the cavernous space it could barely be heard. She looked around. The plane sat silently, like a giant white fly on the floor of a big house. "Scott," she said a little louder, taking tentative steps toward the plane.

A man came out from behind the giant bird. "Who are you calling?" he asked. He wore coveralls and had white hair. He was wiping his hands on a shrimp-colored cloth.

"Scott Thomas."

"Up there." He indicated the plane and turned back to whatever he'd been doing before she came in.

Diana looked at where up there was. She walked around the plane and saw the stairs against the fuselage. Scott was inside the plane. Diana took the steps one at a time. She went inside, standing in the middle of the floor and looking first in one direction, then in the other. She'd logged over a million miles in the last five years, been on countless types of aircrafts, DC-10s, crop dusters and 787s, but this plane, except for its scale, could rival Air Force One.

Taking a few steps to her right, she came upon a lounge complete with curved seating, ambience lighting, big-screen television, a desk and chairs. The whole place looked like something out of *Star Trek:* futuristic, functional and designed for comfort. Her breath escaped, and she put a hand to her mouth to keep it from totally leaving her without air. She'd made a huge amount of money from her business enterprise, but she could not afford one engine of this superplane.

She heard a noise behind her and jumped as if she'd been caught doing something wrong. Scott stood there. He wore a pilot's uniform. Diana had never seen him in it. He looked strong and confident, as if he belonged in it.

"Scott," she said, her mouth dry. She wanted to apologize, but didn't know where to begin. She hadn't expected this environment. She expected to be on the ground. This was like being in some futuristic paradise.

"What are you doing here?"

Diana dropped her arms. "I came to apologize."

"For not returning my phone calls?" He came forward.

She wanted to move back, but felt rooted to the floor. "Yes," she said. "But not only that. I need to apologize for doubting you. I know about Linda Tisdale. I know she was the voice on the other end of the phone and not Linda Engles. You left me to go and save a life. I feel so guilty."

Scott came and stood directly in front to her. He slipped his arm around her waist and pulled her against him. Together they gazed into each other's eyes.

"I didn't meet Linda that day," Scott said. "I know you saw us, but what happened didn't really happen."

Diana didn't say anything. She let Scott go on and explain.

"I ran into her at the coffee shop. I was hoping to run into you." He paused a moment. Diana had intentionally looked for him at the coffee shop when the light turned red. She had not expected to find him kissing Linda.

"It was a friendship kiss," he said as if he could read her thoughts. "We decided that our chance at a relationship had come and gone." He looked at her a long while, his eyes traveling over her as if he needed to take in every detail of her features. "I'm glad you're here," he said.

"Me, too. I've missed you terribly."

"I can't tell you how hard it was for me not to run across this floor and haul you into my arms. It's felt like years since I held you."

"Maybe we could make up for it now," Diana said.

Scott's eyes narrowed. After a moment he moved away from her and went to a wall. Pressing it in a certain place, it opened and a panel came forward. Using a code known to him, Diana heard a motor begin to whir. The sound was muted. Scott looked away from her and she realized he was closing the door of the plane.

"Are we going somewhere?" she asked.

"Oh, yes," he said, his head nodding at the same time. When the door was secured, he closed the panel and returned to her. Taking her hand, he said, "Let me show you around."

They got as far as the bedroom before the tour ended.

* * *

A week later Teddy called Diana to take over a wedding. The consultant, Renee, had gone home ill. Teddy had another wedding to do, and everyone else was busy.

"Don't worry about it," she told Teddy. "I'll get right on it."

"What are you getting right on?" Scott asked when she hung up the phone."

"Come on," she told him. "We're going to a wedding."

"Really? Whose?"

"You don't know them."

Within a few moments, Diana was at the bride's house and filling in for the missing consultant. The bride understood, but her mother wasn't sure she wanted the change.

"I assure you, every detail will be promptly accomplished," Diana assured her. "I've done this many times, and Renee is not at her best. You wouldn't want the bride or groom to become ill on their honeymoon."

That got her. She smiled. And the day began. The prewedding photos were done and they proceeded to the church. Diana rushed to complete everything and make sure everyone was ready.

When the bride started her walk down the aisle Diana was relieved. As she had promised, everything went well.

This was the part of the ceremony she liked best. The couple were about to begin a new life. And today was the beginning of it. They had everything going for them. Diana moved to the side. Scott, in the last pew, slid over to give her room. She slipped into the seat beside him. He smiled at her and took her hand.

"Are you done now?" he whispered.

She nodded. For this wedding, her responsibilities ended after the ceremony. The photos and reception were being handled by someone else. Still, Diana liked to stay until the end.

"We're invited to the reception, and I agreed to attend," she whispered.

The minister was at the part where the couple pledged their troths. Diana had looked that up once to understand what it meant. In today's language, they were pledging their lives to each other before these witnesses and the Divine. This part made her eyes misty whenever she had time to sit down and listen to the words.

Holding Scott's hand made the words seem more personal. She wasn't sure why. She hadn't thought of marrying, ever. She had no time for a husband and a family. Both required a lot of time, and she was not interested in a long-term relationship. But the two of them sitting side by side, holding hands and listening to the wedding vows, made Diana think she might like one day to be floating down the aisle on her way to a new life.

"You may kiss the bride," the minister was saying as Diana returned her attention to the front of the church. For some reason she looked at Scott. His attention was on her, and she knew they both were remembering the kiss they had shared at the altar. Although it was at a rehearsal, that made it no less significant in her mind.

The entire congregation stood. The happy couple started up the aisle, wide smiles on their faces. As they approached Diana and Scott, she turned toward them. Scott stepped forward and pushed his arms around her waist, aligning her body with his. Diana forced herself not to gasp or let her weight sag into his body as it wanted to do.

The bridal party came next, followed by the guests. Diana didn't move. She stayed in Scott's arms. Eventually her head fell back on his shoulder and he kissed her neck. A spiral of electricity went through her with a shock as unexpected as her waking up floating on a boat in the middle of the ocean. She was unprepared, ignorant as to how to proceed. She needed help, and it appeared Scott was right behind her, supporting her, providing her with what she needed keep her body upright.

"Shall we go?" he asked. "Or would you like to be kissed in a church for the third time?"

His words pushed her out of his arms, and she stepped into the aisle. Scott caught her hand. They were the last to leave the sanctuary. The bridal party was coming in from the back to begin their photo session.

"Do you like attending all these weddings?" Scott asked.

"I do," she said, suddenly realizing the double entendre of her reply. Covering herself, she went on: "Giving a bride the perfect day makes me feel…" She stopped. They reached her SUV and both climbed in.

"Go on," Scott prompted. "What do you feel?"

"I feel as if I've fulfilled her greatest wish. Sometimes the groom's, too."

"Don't you ever want that for yourself?"

Diana was unprepared for the question. "I never really thought about it." She was driving, but she looked aside, trying to find out where he was going with this.

"I know you aren't looking for a long-term relationship. But since you attend several weddings a year, don't you ever think of it being you in the bridal gown?"

Strange he should bring this up. She'd been thinking that exact thing only minutes ago, as they sat holding hands.

"Once or twice," she admitted.

"Yet you are in a field where the men you meet are on their way to the altar."

"There are the groomsmen," she quipped. "Not all of them are taken."

Scott remained quiet for a moment. In the wedding they had just left, several of the groomsmen were in her age bracket and unattached.

"But you went to MatchforLove.com. Why is that?"

She frowned. Scott leaned forward and looked at her from the passenger seat.

"While there are single men at these weddings, I'm very busy, and most of the ones I meet are either engaged or obnoxious," Diana answered.

"Like me?" he finished for her.

"Like you." Her smile took the sting out of the words. It felt good to be able to laugh at that now.

"I didn't go to MatchforLove.com on my own," she finally said. "Teddy convinced me to go."

"Why?"

Diana sighed. She wasn't sure she wanted to tell Scott the full story, but there was no reason not to. "Getting a business off the ground takes a lot of work," Diana said. Scott nodded. "I've been working night and day for years trying to get the business to support itself. Every ounce of energy I had went into making my wedding planning franchise a success. Consequently, I have no time for singles bars, cafés or blind dates. Coaxed by Teddy, one night I went into MatchforLove.com and filled out the questionnaire. I didn't expect anything to come of it. Even if it did, I was not obligated to respond."

"Why did you respond to me? My profile reads nothing like yours. I didn't leave a photo, so you only had a numeric email address."

"I read what you were looking for in a woman. It was as if you'd read my mind. I thought I'd see if that was true."

"Have you made a decision yet?"

"Let's just say the jury is still out on that."

Diana reached the reception hall and pulled into the crowded parking lot. She parked near the entrance to the parking lot. It was a method of advertising. People driving by would see the SUV and the advertising on the side doors. Since Diana had no responsibilities here, she didn't need to have access to the equipment and materials she took to every wedding. However, if something happened that she could fix, she'd do it.

Ahead of them, a couple got out of their car, along with the two young flower girls.

Diana smiled at them in their perfect little pink-and-white dresses.

"Cute, right?" Scott asked, following her line of vision.

"Jacey and Merry." She told him the girls' names, spelling Merry's.

"She was born during the Christmas holidays?" Scott stated.

Diana nodded. "December twenty-third."

They watched as Merry's dad came up and took both girls' hands.

"I suppose with your business that's not in your future, either."

"What?" Diana asked.

"A husband and kids? They take a lot of time."

"It's a bridge, Scott."

"Bridge?"

"As in one I don't have to cross at this moment. Children change your life."

"Are you saying yours will change? You'll be able to let someone else manage your empire while you play homemaker?"

"Maybe, maybe not. At least while I breast-feed, I suppose I could release the reins." She knew it was the wrong thing to say the moment the words left her lips. Scott's eyes went straight to her breasts.

"Marriage isn't on my mind. As I remember it, you said you weren't interested in a relationship."

"I guess that means we're even."

"Maybe. Maybe not," he quoted her. "Remember that uncertainty principle we learned about in school?"

"What does that have to do with us?"

"You never know when something will happen to change your life. You could fall in love tomorrow. And that could change everything you thought you wanted. The time line you think you own would be cut and pasted down on another road."

"Anybody I know on that road?" Diana wanted to lighten the mood. Somehow they had gotten onto a subject that said more by what was not being said than by the actual words.

"Maybe…maybe not."

Scott had been away overnight. He'd had to fly the corporate jet and several executives to a meeting. They were back. He'd be on the ground in ten minutes. He started his descent into the Princeton area. This height always reminded him of his dad. When he started to come down from the heavens and the earth was no longer somewhere under the clouds. When the trees began to fill in and you could see the green, but not define any roads or houses. It looked like rural Maine, where he learned to fly. Soon he'd see the lights of the city ahead. Usually there was nothing waiting for him except an empty hotel room and a paperback novel. Today Diana would be there. He couldn't wait to get to her. He wanted to run through the airport and scoop her into his arms, rain kisses on her face until she could do nothing but laugh and return them.

But there were formalities first. He shut down the plane's engine, and the attendants opened the doors. There was no ambulance waiting, but there were certain measures required by the FAA. The ground crew took care of them. Scott left his bag, which hadn't been opened during this trip and went into the gate area.

He saw Diana the moment he walked into the small airport. She started toward him. His legs moved, and they were running toward each other as if they hadn't seen each other in years instead of the few hours they'd been apart. He liked seeing her there, liked knowing that she waited for him. He finally understood his friends when they talked about having someone to come home to. He could see himself coming home to her.

Her smile was wide and her arms were out. He closed his around her and swung her around. Then he kissed her in full view of anyone present. Slipping his arm around her waist, he started walking toward the exit.

"Miss me?" he asked.

"Not much." She laughed.

He loved that laugh. He loved everything about her.

"What did you do while I was gone?"

"I sold another franchise."

"That's wonderful. Tell me about it."

"It's in Denver. And that means I'll have to make several trips there over the next few months."

"Aren't you lucky that you know someone with an airplane?"

He only had a flight bag and didn't need to wait for luggage. The business provided him with transportation to and from the airport, but today he preferred to go with her.

"Where shall I drop you?" she asked as they went to her car.

"You didn't come all the way out here to take me home," he told her.

"It's not that far." She flashed him that smile that gave meaning to his day. The top was down and her hair flew about in the sunshine. Scott kept his hands down so he wouldn't run them through it and possibly cause an accident.

"I have news for you."

"Oh, good or bad?"

He frowned. "I'm not sure."

She glanced at him, seeing the confusion on his face.

"My sister is coming to visit. Well, she's coming for a meeting in Philly, but she wants to come up one night and have dinner."

"That's great. It's good to keep in touch with family. Are you two very close?"

"Thick as thieves," he said. "But she's not coming to see me. She wants to have dinner with you."

Diana looked at him as long as the road would allow. "Why?"

"I told her about you."

"What did you say?" Her tone was cautious.

"Only good things."

They reached the turnoff for her house before they got to his. Diana turned right and parked in her driveway.

"When should I expect this visit?" she asked.

"Next week."

As soon as she stopped the car, the July heat made its withering effect felt. Inside the air was cool and comfortable. Scott took Diana in his arms and kissed her soundly.

"I've thought about that for two days," he said.

"Then you should do it again. One for each day."

He did. She smelled of jasmine soap and sweet skin. Scott kissed her deeply. He slipped his arms around her and pulled her slender body into his. He'd missed her more than he wanted to admit. Scott had spent all the time except that of flying the plane thinking about her and what he wanted to do with her. Diana's arms climbed over his shoulders and she joined him in the kiss. It was a long time before they parted.

"I love this dress," Scott told her. He touched the spaghetti straps on her shoulders and pushed them down her arms.

"Why?"

"Because all I need to do is release this zipper." He pulled it from the top to its base. He listened to low crunch of the teeth coming apart. "And it falls off."

"Unlike your clothes," she said, unbuttoning the top button on his shirt. "It takes a lot to get you out of them." With each word she released a button until they were all open. She pulled his tie from his neck and draped it around her own.

Scott bent and kissed her. Her bra was strapless, and his fingers found and released the catch at the back. Her breasts were caught in his hands. Her skin was soft and warm, and Scott wanted to take her there. Diana's hands, on the belt at his waist, stilled as sensation burst within her. Hooking her fingers in the waistband of his pants, Diana pushed them down. He stepped out of his shoes and the clothes pooled at his feet.

Scott kissed her neck and continued finding naked skin until he reached her breasts. As his tongue lathed her nipples, they tightened and stiffened. Scott had been away only two days, but he couldn't wait any longer for Diana. And from the way she was climbing over him, she couldn't wait, either.

Chapter 11

The main street of Princeton wasn't very long. Except for the students who came and went with the semester changes, it was impossible to live there and not see the same people constantly. So when Diana spied Linda Engles going into the coffee shop, she knew it was time to talk to her.

She'd been angry when she spoke to Linda in the ladies' room, but Diana refused to be vindictive like Linda. And she would not hold a sword over her. Ordering a coffee, she strolled over to Linda's table. She was reading a newspaper and sipping a latte.

"May I sit down?" Diana asked.

Linda looked up and did a double take. She said nothing as Diana took the seat in front of her.

"What do you want?" Linda's voice was fearful and her eyes darted around the coffee shop checking if they were within hearing distance of anyone.

"I'm not here to make a scene," Diana told her. "Or to issue threats."

Linda folded the paper and turned in the seat to fully face Diana. She knew the woman expected some type of altercation, despite Diana's words.

"I'm here to apologize."

Linda's face contorted into a skeptical frown. "I don't understand."

"That night in the ladies' room, I said some pretty terrible things."

Linda nodded. Her face was ghostly white.

"I was very rude. I said some things, issued some threats. I just want to say, you don't have to worry that I would ever use any of that information."

"Wh-why?" she stuttered.

"That's not who I am. I was angry, *very* angry that night. I've been taunted and ridiculed for years and I was no longer able to control how I felt. But I am not a blackmailer. I will keep your secret as long as you want. You need have no fear that anything related to your past will cross my lips."

It took Linda a while to be able to speak. She seemed to be lost for whatever the words were she needed. "I don't understand," she said. "You have a bombshell. You could detonate my life if you wanted. I know I shouldn't ask this, but why are you willing to keep it a secret?"

Diana smiled. "It's not my place to reveal other people's secrets. It reflects badly on me. I operate a business. One that runs on reputation. I don't want my reputation tarnished, just as you don't want yours tarnished. You made a mistake years ago—why should you pay for it the rest of your life?"

"I don't understand you."

Diana smiled. "That's all right."

"But I treated you so badly. For years I belittled you."

"But if I continue that kind of behavior, it only makes me an offender."

Linda looked at her for a long, long moment. "Thank you," she finally whispered.

Diana could feel the weight that had lifted from Linda's shoulders. Diana got up to leave. Linda called her back. "Can I buy you a cup of coffee?"

"For old time's sake?" Diana smiled.

Linda shook her head. "For all the new times."

It was rare for Scott to wait for a passenger to get off a plane, but he stood waiting for Piper to deplane. She'd called the day before to say she was flying into Princeton and wanted to see him.

Piper was attending a meeting in Philadelphia and would make a small detour to see him. Of course the real person she wanted to see was Diana. Scott had told her a lot about Diana, and it was natural for his sister to want to meet her. When Piper met her husband, Scott arranged to be in a nearby town so he could meet him. After her first marriage failed, he was concerned that she wouldn't make a good choice this time. Not that he would have told her if she hadn't. Scott knew the limits even with family. If she was about to make a mistakes, she had to see it for herself. Scott knew nothing was foretold. There was no way he or anyone could assess the success of a marriage. But when he met Josh Winesap, he liked him immediately. Since then the two men had been the best of friends. And Piper never mentioned him without a smile on her face or a lilt in her voice.

Scott's mouth dropped open when he saw his obviously pregnant sister deplane. She smiled and waved to him. As she came into the terminal and directly into his arms, he hugged her close, feeling her protruding belly.

"When did this happen?" he asked pushing her back and giving her a brotherly once-over.

"Several months ago."

"And with all the emails and phone calls, you didn't

think this was important to mention?" Still holding her hands, he raised them and looked at her again.

"We didn't want to tell anyone until the first trimester ended." Putting her hands on her belly, she looked down. "Five months next week."

"You don't have to tell anyone now. They can see." He hugged her again. "Congratulations. You're going to be a wonderful mom."

"And you're going to be a great uncle."

"Have you told Mom and Dad yet?"

She rolled her eyes. "It took an hour to convince them they didn't need to fly up here and take care of me."

Scott laughed, and together they left the terminal.

"So when do I meet her?" Piper said.

Scott didn't pretend not to know who she meant. "I thought you were coming to see me."

"I've seen you. Now when do I get to see Diana?"

"You say that as if you're here to approve of her. We're not even seeing each other."

"Scott, I've heard you discuss jet engines, beating hearts, flying in bad weather, skimming tree tops and a myriad of other subjects. Rarely have you discussed a woman. Yet you've told me more about Diana Greer than any other person in ten years. And even back then you mentioned her a time or two. So yes, I want to meet her. But no, I'm not here to approve. Just hope."

"Hope? What does that mean?"

"It means I hope she's the one for you."

Scott looked at the ceiling even though he was driving. "Not you, too."

"'Me too' what?"

"My buddies."

"Not the ones from the Wall."

"Not them. These are guys I went to college with. They

all know Diana and staged, for want of a better word, an intervention."

Piper's head whipped around.

"They didn't kidnap me or anything like that. They just showed up for lunch one day with a lot of questions about me and Diana."

"You and Diana as a couple."

Scott nodded. He didn't trust himself to speak. The idea of a couple had been on his mind, but he'd suppressed thinking about it. Neither he nor Diana was looking for a relationship, especially a long-term one. It was the one question both of them had answered no to on their profiles. Yet he enjoyed being with her. Obviously his sister thought the same thing.

"Are you a couple?" Piper continued.

"We are not."

"Do I hear a *yet* at the end of that sentence?"

"You do not. Both of us were looking for companionship, not a lifemate."

"Things change." She sang the words, an impish smile on her mouth.

The gales of laughter coming from the three women was not what Scott had expected when he walked into the bar. In fact, he didn't expect them to be in the bar. He'd dropped Piper at the restaurant, and she was, at her request, to have dinner with Diana. No one said Teddy would be there, too. Scott started for the table. The three women raised glasses and clinked them together before drinking and again bursting into laughter.

He felt defensive. He didn't know what Piper could be telling them, but he had the paranoid feeling that he was the subject of their regalia.

"What's going on?" Scott asked as he reached the table.

The women answered by bursting into laughter.

"Piper, I hope you haven't been airing the family laundry."

She raised her hand for him to wait until she could stop laughing and get herself under control.

"You can relax," Teddy said. "You're not the subject of discussion."

Scott took the only empty chair at the table. "Who is?"

"I am," Diana said.

"Diana and Teddy have been telling me about some of the things that happened at the weddings they've consulted."

The giggles got to them again, and one by one the three joined into laughter on a joke that he was not privy to. Scott checked the table. There were several wineglasses strewn about and a candle that had burned nearly to its base. "How much have you guys had to drink?" Scott looked directly at his sister's glass.

"Mineral water," she told him.

"I don't remember," Teddy said.

"I'm driving," Diana finished, taking a drink of the dark-colored liquid in her glass.

"So what were some of the wedding stories?"

The question was simple, but again it seemed the three women had lost their ability to speak. Laughter replaced all other forms of communication.

"Diana told us about the troll," Piper finally said.

Diana and Teddy nodded.

"She was a short woman. Pretty and petite, but she'd been to a bridal fashion show and saw a pintucked dress she had to have. It was... Well, let's just say it was something that Scarlett from *Gone with the Wind* could have worn. It was designed for a much taller woman, but she kept adding things to it: a hat, veil, very high heels. And then the umbrella."

"Umbrella?"

"After adding all that stuff, she looked like a troll."

Scott didn't find that funny. "I guess you had to be there," he said.

"I guess so."

After he and Diana stared at each other for a long moment, Piper spoke up. "I hate to cut this short. It's been great." She stood up and pushed her chair in. "I have to sit all day in that meeting tomorrow, so I'd better get to bed."

"We'll do this again," Teddy stated.

"We'll have to," Piper smiled. Each woman stood and hugged Piper. The party broke up and they all headed for the door.

Scott let Teddy lead. She and Piper were in conversation when he took Diana's arm. "What did you really talk about?" he asked.

"We wouldn't lie to you, Scott. We talked about weddings, flying airplanes. You didn't tell me she's a pilot, too. And of course, the most important thing. We talked about you, *Skippy*."

She stood on her toes, planted a kiss on his nose and joined the two women ahead of them. Scott didn't take the kiss as sexual. It was more of an I've-got-a-secret kiss. He wondered what his sister had said. Like Linda, he expected the two women would be like oil and water, or at the least have a standoff. Coming into the restaurant and finding them deep in laughter, looking as if they'd known each other for years, was totally unexpected.

Piper didn't trust easily and apparently neither did Diana, yet the two got on as if they'd played in the same sandbox. And she'd told Diana about Skippy. Scott's dad had told him not to try and understand women. They only changed if you got anywhere near figuring them out.

Today he understood the truth of that statement.

The air was perfect for flying. The wind speed wasn't too strong or too weak. The sky was clear, and Scott was waiting for Diana. He'd invited her to the airfield but had not told her why or where they were going. Emerging from the Porsche, Scott watched her walk to the hangar. Dressed in a pair of pants and a light jacket, she was the picture of sunshine as she strolled across the tarmac. Her hair was pulled back in a ponytail, and she slipped the sunglasses from her crown to cover her eyes.

He stepped out from behind the plane. She smiled when she saw him coming.

"Is this your plane?" Diana asked when she was within speaking distance.

Scott glanced at the plane. He nodded. "My father gave it to me when I graduated from college."

"Most people get interview clothes. I guess this worked as a luggage carrier." She folded her arms and smiled at him. "And you needed some way to get to Montana."

"Naturally," he said.

"Are we going inside?"

He started walking toward the stairs. "I thought we'd go for a ride."

"Where?" Diana asked.

"How about Washington, D.C.? Or Maine?"

She turned on the stairs and looked at him. "Maine?"

"It's not that far. You don't have any wedding planned. You have no franchise appointments. According to Teddy, you're free for a couple of days."

"So Teddy is in on this?"

He nodded. "You should never go anywhere without filing a flight plan."

"And she's mine?"

"She's yours."

After a moment she moved all the way up and stepped through the door. Scott followed, watching her as she looked around the space. The plane seated ten. All the seats were empty. She turned back and looked at him.

"I don't have any clothes."

"I don't think you'll need any." He smiled.

"It might be cold in Maine," she said, a blush painting up from her neck and into her face.

"We have blankets."

"Then I guess I'm out of excuses."

Offering her his hand, she slowly walked toward him and placed her hand in his. Scott led her to the cockpit. He settled her in the copilot's seat and showed her how to put on her headphones.

"Are you sure I should sit here?"

"As long as you don't take the controls, you'll be fine."

He put his headphones on and checked with the tower. After a few routine comments he was cleared. And the two were on their way.

"When did you decide you wanted to be a pilot?" Diana asked several minutes later after they were no longer over the recognizable portions of the state. She had to talk into the microphone for Scott to hear her.

"It wasn't something I decided. It just happened."

"How? Who taught you?"

"My father. He's northern Maine's answer to the bush pilot."

"Really? You're from Maine?"

Scott shook his head. "I grew up in Minnesota. My parents have a house in Maine. We used to go up there every summer. The house is in a remote part of the state. My dad and I would hunt and talk, and he'd take me flying. I think the first time I had the controls in my hands, I was eight years old."

He smiled and Diana could tell he'd lapsed into a happy childhood memory.

"Just holding those controls was like…like nothing I'd ever felt before. I had this big airplane, and with the smallest movement of my hands, it would do what I wanted. The rush I felt was like nothing I could describe. From that moment on, I wanted to fly." He laughed, again at some past memory. "I pestered my dad every minute to let me do it again. I had my pilot's license by the time I was sixteen. I could fly a plane before I could drive a car."

"Did you always fly corporate planes?"

"Other than my dad's planes, I tried a few with the big airlines." His tone told her he hadn't been thrilled.

"Didn't you like it?"

"I didn't like the routine. I had a route. It was like flying all day and going nowhere. I much prefer the corporate jets."

"Nonroutine, I take it?"

"I guess that's part of it. It also allows me a lot of free time. There isn't a flight every day or sometimes twice a day."

"With the world doing email and telecommunicating, is there that much call for a corporate plane, or is it a prestige thing?"

"There's still enough call for in-person meetings, but I'm sure it's prestigious to have your own plane. You can go when you want instead of having to rush things because the last plane out leaves at a specific time."

"Is your dad still alive?"

"Both parents are alive and well and living in Minnesota. My dad is semiretired. He works three days a week, still flies his own plane and operates a ground school for pilots.

"What about you? Did you always want to be a wedding consultant?"

"I'm not a consultant. I run a franchise."

"Excuse me." He winced, as if he'd said something wrong. "Did you always want to own a wedding business? There were no courses like that at Princeton, unless I missed them."

"How would you know," she smiled shyly. "Your major was female anatomy. And that wasn't in the curriculum, either."

"It was not." He pretended to be hurt. "And if I had, I see you were quite knowledgeable to what I was doing."

"You were always in my way, always had a woman on your arm. That is until Linda knocked them all aside."

He dropped his eyes. "Yeah, Linda," he said.

Diana didn't know how to read into that. She decided not to pursue it. Linda Engles latched on to Scott like a leech and the campus gossip had them marrying when they graduated. Even though Diana hadn't seen Scott since leaving the university, her heart sang that he hadn't tied himself to a woman like Linda.

"Your turn," Scott said. "How did you get into weddings? Your major was either mathematics or computer science, wasn't it?"

"Both. I had a double major and double minor," Diana corrected him. "One of my minors was business. I always knew I wanted to own my own business. I didn't know what kind. Then my sister announced her engagement."

"You have a sister?"

"Joselyn." She nodded. "I also have two brothers. Twins."

Scott gazed at her as if memorizing her features. There was so much he didn't know. He'd never taken the time when they were in college. Now he wanted to know everything about her.

"Where do you fit in the mix?"

"I'm in the middle. Brothers are older, sister younger."

"Anyway, Joselyn announced her engagement and asked me to be her wedding consultant. I'd never done it before, and she couldn't afford to hire one. I was good at organization and details, so I agreed to do it."

"And you found your calling?"

"Sort of. The wedding was rife with changes. The groom's mother hated everything. Although she's come to love my sister, she was a force to be reckoned with during the planning process. The bridesmaids argued, and one left the wedding party. I felt like I was always putting down an argument."

"Then what made you go into the business?"

"The day of the wedding, it was like all the pieces fell into place. The bride was beautiful; the groom was gorgeous and in love. The parents were proud. The church was decorated with fragrant flowers. The cake was delivered on time and exactly what the bride requested. I cried during the ceremony."

"You cried," he teased.

"She's my baby sister. And she never looked lovelier."

Scott saw Diana blink a couple of times, warding off the tears women sometimes shed when they were happy.

"When the ceremony was over and all the photos had been taken," she went on, "when the dancing ended and the bouquet was thrown and we'd seen the couple off to their honeymoon and the beginning of their life together, it all seemed worth it."

She glanced at Scott who was hanging on every word,

as if she was telling a timeless story that had been passed from generation to generation for unknown ages. "I know it sounds strange, but I wanted so much to do it again."

"It doesn't sound strange."

"I made up some business cards and went around to bridal and tuxedo shops and left my cards. A few weeks later I got a call, and that's when it began."

"Was the second wedding as complicated as your sister's?"

She shook her head. "I suppose if it had been, I might have changed my mind about a profession. I like doing the weddings, making the bride's day the most wonderful of her life."

Scott smiled at her. The expression on her face had a glow to it. She truly loved what she did, but he wondered about her choice. He knew her to be an introvert. It was strange to see this outgoing, afraid-of-no-one woman in front of him.

But as a wedding consultant or even as a business owner, she'd barred herself from the happiness that could be hers. Diana had put herself in a place where everyone she met was taken or about to be taken. Scott wondered if she did that on purpose. Was she intentionally trying to avoid meeting people?

And how much had his actions played into that decision?

Maine came into view an hour later. Twenty minutes after that Scott was setting the plane down on the airfield about a hundred yards from the house.

Diana stopped as she came through the cockpit door. She walked three steps down and stared at the house. "You said this was a cabin."

Scott was behind her, but she never took her eyes off the distant house.

Scott glanced at the house and back at Diana. "It is."

"Look at the size of this place. It's a small hotel."

He looked at the timber-log building with its solar-paneled roof, huge windows and wraparound porch. "I suppose it is a little large. Initially it was being built for sales meetings, but after construction began my father decided the location was too remote, so he had it converted to a summer home. Let's go in."

Diana went down the stairs to the ground.

"What's that?"

She looked at the two overnight bags he was carrying. He lifted hers. "Your flight plan."

"How'd you get that?"

"Teddy. She packed a bag for you. I don't think you should spend the weekend completely naked."

They headed for the house.

"How many bedrooms does this place have?"

"I think there are fifteen. I haven't counted them in years."

"It is a hotel," Diana muttered.

They walked the short distance and went up the stairs to the porch. Scott opened the polished wood door.

"Have you been here recently?" Diana asked, when they stepped inside. The smell of furniture polish was evident.

"I hired a caretaker last week. The place has been aired and cleaned, and there should be food in the kitchen."

"I guess going to the corner store could be a problem."

The place was warm. But even in July, the air would chill after sundown. Diana walked to the fireplace in the large open room. The fire had been laid, but not lit. On the mantel was a box of long matches. She turned the flue to open, then she lit the paper and the fire began.

"Are you hungry?" he asked. She shook her head. They both headed for the sofa that flanked the fireplace. "Would you like a tour?"

She nodded. Scott reached for her hand. She took it and he pulled her close. They went from room to room on the first level. The place was large enough to hold meetings. Scott had never thought about the size of it, but from Diana's perspective, someone who'd grown up in a semi-detached house in Philadelphia, this place was gargantuan.

"Wow!" Diana said when they went into the kitchen. "It's a dream." She turned to Scott. "In my next life I'm going to be a designer. I'll specialize in kitchens."

"Does that mean you can cook?"

"I've been known to boil water without burning the pot." She walked over and opened one of the restaurant-size refrigerators. "How many people did you tell this caretaker to plan for?" The place had everything a person could even think of wanting to eat.

Scott reached over her and grabbed a small bottle of orange juice. Twisting off the cap, he drank half of it.

Diana closed the door. "This place is very remote," she said. "What happens if someone becomes ill or needs assistance?"

Taking her arm, he led her to an outside wall. "This is a satellite phone. It has a solar charger. There are several of them posted around the area. They're in red boxes and attached to trees. There's also a shortwave radio in the den." He looked back toward the other side of the house. "I'll show you how it works later."

"I see your father thought of everything."

"More my mother," he said. "She insisted that we needed to be able to reach help if he was going to have people here."

"Who do we call on these satellite phones?"

"The forest service. Numbers are next to each phone. They know we're here."

"Again, the flight plan?" she asked.

"Safety first," he replied.

They continued the tour, finally leaving the first floor and walking through the many bedrooms and bathrooms on the second level. Scott counted as they went. Other than the master suite, there were fifteen other bedrooms and ten bathrooms.

"Which one of these rooms is yours?"

"The one with the dark red bedspread."

"Maroon," Diana corrected.

"Yeah, that one."

"Which one is mine?"

"Anyone you want," he said. "You have a number to choose from."

"Maroon," she said.

"Good choice."

Chapter 12

While Scott made the fire, Diana found her way around the state-of-the-art kitchen. Her mother taught all her children to cook, even the twins. Diana smiled, thinking of how she would tell them, "You always have to eat." She didn't require them to learn fancy meals, just basic food. Diana had branched out, and during the lean years of getting her business off the ground, she'd taught herself quite a few recipes.

Tonight she put those lessons to work. She tossed a salad, made glazed carrots, found frozen peas in the freezer and added a thick steak, which she cooked on the smokeless broiler. She even baked some fresh biscuits. The kitchen had a vast amount of spices, and these she used to enhance the steak and the salad. There was a wine cooler near the refrigerator. She found a bottle of red wine, and finding the dining room table formidably long, she opted to set a small circular table in the den.

"Smells good in here," Scott said, coming through the door. He looked at the wine bottle sitting on the counter. "Shall I open this?"

She nodded. After a few minutes, the food was on the table and they were sitting down to eat.

"I must say I'm surprised. For a woman who owns her own business, I never really expected that you would know how to cook."

"Reserve your judgment," she teased. "You haven't tasted it yet."

Scott took a spoon and dipped it in the carrots. Diana smacked his hand before he could put it in his mouth.

"I'll bet your mom used to do that."

"And I'll bet your cook used to do that to you."

"She did."

"The steaks are rare at the moment. How do you like yours?"

"Medium," he replied. Moments later they were seated at the table with the food before them. Scott ate as if this was the best meal he'd ever had.

"Like it?" Diana asked.

"I didn't realize how long it's been since I had a home-cooked meal."

"How long has it been?" she asked, as they moved to the kitchen to clean up.

"I guess the last time was when Piper had Thanksgiving at her house."

"Thanksgiving was four months ago."

"Not last Thanksgiving, the one before."

Diana frowned. "I suppose I'll have to eat bad food in the morning, right?"

"Why?" he asked.

"I cooked dinner, breakfast is your job. And I want something worthy of the chefs at the Waldorf Astoria."

"Room service." Scott grinned at her, and Diana knew that smile had more in it than the discussion of food.

Taking their wine, they moved to the sofa in front of the fire he'd built. "It's lovely here," Diana said. She looked up at the high ceiling in the room. "It reminds me of a ski lodge I went to once in Lake Tahoe."

"Do you ski?"

"No." She shook her head. "Do you?"

"Never learned. Never wanted to. You can't ski here, anyway. It's too secluded. Landing a plane here in the winter is dangerous. The runway has too much snow on it, and no one can get here to clear it."

Diana lowered her head to his shoulder. "It must be beautiful here in the winter."

Scott put his arm around her and she cuddled into the crook of it. The fire snapped and crackled.

"Glad you came?" he whispered. She felt his mouth move above her head.

"It's very relaxing. The scenery is good. And the company can be tolerated."

He laughed, his body moving against her. "Who knew Brainiac had a sense of humor?" His hands smoothed her hair. "Do you mind me calling you that? I don't mean it in a sarcastic way."

She shook her head. "I kind of like it, but only when you say it."

Scott turned her head up to look at her. His eyes were dark and filled with need. He set his glass on the sofa table behind them. Then took hers and placed it next to his. She twisted in his arms and watched his movements. When his eyes came back to hers, he ran his hand down the back of her head and pulled her mouth to his. The kiss was soft, tender, loving. Diana went willingly into his arms. She could say the wine led her to it, but that wasn't the truth. She loved this man. She wanted to be here, wanted to be in his arms with him wrapped around her.

The sofa was one of those circular numbers that had been designed to go with the curved well it set in. Scott

pushed her back until she was lying under him. He deep-
ened the kiss, and Diana almost lost her breath with the
way her body reacted to his. She wanted to devour him,
wanted to crawl all over and pull him into her. She wanted
the pleasure of lying naked with him and waking with the
warmth of his body surrounding her.

She pulled at his clothes, divesting him of his shirt and
pants. Her own clothes followed his as Scott touched her.
She felt her body tremble beneath his hands. Her breasts
were freed and he quickly covered them, first with his
hands, then with his mouth. Diana gasped at the wetness of
his first touch. Then she reveled in the feel of him, holding
his head and arching her back so he could give her more
and more of himself.

Her eyes closed as his hands caressed her. He kissed
her all over, his mouth touching and tasting every part
of her. Diana felt the heat of him. Her hands sought him,
roved over his smooth skin. She kissed his shoulders, his
pecs, feeling his nipples harden in her mouth. Fire burned
in her fingers as they journeyed down his back and over
his buttocks. His body was toned, hard from working out.
His waist nipped in as she brought her hands around him
and took his penis in her palms. Using both her thumbs,
she ran them across the hardness, feeling the hard ridge
and throb of his need.

Scott groaned at her touch, but didn't move to stop her.
She continued what she knew was an exquisite torture. She
watched him. His eyes were closed and his face showed
that he enjoyed the feel of her hands. In a lightning-fast
movement, he switched positions with her, turning her
over on the sofa and beginning the same kind of torture
she was inflicting on him. He covered himself with a condom almost at the same time he covered her with his artis-
tic body. Spreading her legs, he entered her. Diana pulled

him in, closed around him in a position so tight it said she would keep him there for all time.

But there was no time. Clocks did not exist in this world. They could go on forever, and when they returned not a second would have advanced on any chronometer.

Diana moved beneath Scott. Just the slightest movement causes more pleasure than anyone should be allowed to feel. When Scott pulled back and entered her again, she thought she'd die in the one movement. But he continued. And so sounds came from her. She felt the exertion, felt the pleasure, and she was unable to keep from making a physical sound. Scott's hands pushed into her hair. His mouth took hers in a devastating kiss. His body didn't stop the assault on her senses. Erotic pleasure points emerged from unknown sources.

She melted beneath him. Her hands felt uncontrollable. They raced up and down his back, over the curve of his behind and down powerful legs that were moving up and down as he pushed and pulled inside her. Diana's brain registered no thought. She became only a feeling being. Her body worked with Scott's, as if the two had become a machine that knew the motion of rapture. Passion spiraled between them. Scott held her tighter, his hands on her waist, as he fit his body into hers and out again.

Over and over she accepted his strokes, giving as good as she got. When she felt she could take it no longer, Scott raised the threshold. He pulled her into a sitting position. Her legs straddled him and he pushed into her at a different angle and into a different pleasurable area inside her. Diana sighed, a sound that was not describable. In seconds she was over the edge, trying to force herself not to shout Scott's name and finding it impossible to contain.

Gasping for air, they plunged back to earth. Diana was spent. She clung to Scott, squeezing her legs around him and holding on, as if one or both of them would fall into the open abyss they had created.

Even with ragged breath and a body pounding with the energy of sated sex, Scott's hands roamed Diana's back. He seemed to need to touch her skin, keep her warm with his hands. She loved the feel of him, loved the way he made her feel. She wanted his hands to stay on her for at least the next century. Pushing his fingers up into her hair, he angled her mouth to his and kissed her breathless.

Scott wove his fingers through Diana's hair. She watched his face as he let the strands rain through them, almost as if he was counting them.

Without moving his head or his hand, he turned his eyes to her. Eyes that were soft and hungry. "Promise me you'll never cut your hair."

Diana smiled. "Not even when the style changes to short and chic?"

"You can wear it up, but every night I get to take it down." He bent forward and kissed her forehead, then the tip of her nose and her mouth.

"Not even when I'm old and gray and look like Cousin Itt?"

She meant to get a laugh out him, but his features were soft, but serious.

"Not even then." Again he kissed her. This time deeper, pushing her back into the pillows. "And you're not going to get old and gray."

She pushed him a few inches away. "I'm going to get old and gray."

He shook his head, an impish smile on his mouth. "When we're old we'll dye our hair, you can dye mine and I'll do yours."

"And only our hairdressers will know." They both

laughed at the tagline of a commercial they had watched together on television.

"It's a promise," Diana said.

She reached up and pulled Scott's head down. She kissed his forehead, the tip of his nose and his mouth. At his mouth she lingered, feathering kisses inch by inch from one corner to the other. Her body grew as warm as liquid. She stretched under him, positioning herself so he touched her from breast to knee. His body was hard against her softness. Diana loved the feel of him. She touched his hair, smoothing her hand down his neck and across his shoulder.

Scott's leg crossed hers, pinning her down. Diana welcomed his weight. She felt his erection against her leg. The feel of him had her moving her leg up and down against his. She felt the roughness of his skin. Small flames caught from him to her.

The room seemed to change. It was bright morning, and they'd spent the night in each other's arms. Around them she could smell sex, the electric snap of energy that accompanied their coupling. But beneath that was the combined scents they produced. She not only took in the essence of Scott, but reveled in his taste. His mouth devoured hers with a hunger that was deep with need. Diana found it hard to breathe. Yet she was reluctant to let go. She never wanted to be out of Scott's arms. She was as hungry for him now as she'd been only a few hours ago, before the sun rose, before night turned into a new day, before life began.

He pulled the sheet covering her away and lifted his head to looked at her. His eyes roamed over her breasts. He didn't touch them, although his mouth was only a kiss away. His breath on her skin burned it. Her nipples peaked, straining forward, trying to reach his mouth of their own accord. Diana's chest heaved despite her effort to breathe normally. Around Scott there was no normal. Everything with him was fresh and new.

After what seemed like years, his mouth closed over one nipple. Diana groaned at the pleasure that fissured through her. Her body rose off the mattress, pushing her forward toward the pleasure he promised. She wanted more. The need in her ranked up notches. Diana could no longer hold her voice in. Sounds as guttural and primal as the dawn of time came from her. She moved her body, slipped farther under Scott until he covered her totally. She spread her legs, letting his erection settle in the juncture of her thighs. He touched her sweet spot and she nearly toppled them with the writhing that was electrical and shockingly sensational. It was as if he'd found a new erogenous area that had yearned for discovery, but had never been touched. His throbbing body shocked it into being, and she exploded with pent-up pleasure.

Diana didn't want Scott to separate from her, but he took a second to protect them. Then he was back, as hot as a furnace, as needy as she was. His body seemed to hunger for hers with the same intensity that she craved. In a second he entered her. Her pleasure seekers were out and ready. The touch of him opened all doors. She gasped as he began the timeless rhythm. Diana joined in, her hands on his hips, his body pumping into hers. He rose and pushed. She rose and accepted. Together they made love. Her hands roved over him. His body melded with hers. Sensation as tangible as fire soared through her.

She would grow old with Scott, and when they could hardly walk they could still lay together, be together. They could wrap up in each other's arms and remember the fire, remember the long days ahead and the long nights of lovemaking to come. And they would know the secret. They would know that love, however discovered, in either the universe of computer science or campus tomfoolery would find the two people it needed, and nothing could keep them apart.

Diana didn't think she could go burn up any more, but the sudden rush within and the feral nature of Scott's movements told her that he was beyond control. She didn't think about it. She was burning with his love, and she wanted whatever he would give her. He was beyond holding anything. As was she. Like a tigress stalking her mate, she went with everything she had. Her body took on a life of its own, surging up and taking Scott into her, then holding him for a moment before repeating the act. She went on. Her mouth was dry. Her body was burning. She didn't think she could continue, but the passion she felt, the pleasure of holding him inside her, went higher with each stroke. She kept at it. He kept at it. She wasn't sure if they were trying to outdo each other, but the result was too wonderful for them both.

Finally, she felt the scream coming. It started deep in her body, almost as far down as her toes. Gathering sped and burning like a fireball, it grew into a giant wave that crested at their union. Sound filled the room as their climax exploded. Diana didn't know whose voice it was. The two mingled together at their mutual satisfaction.

Scott fell against her. She was slick and sated. She tasted the salt on her mouth as his head brushed her lips. Ragged breaths came from them both. The sound punctuated the air. Under Scott, she still moved. His stationary body still felt good against her own. She didn't know how she had the energy, but he felt too good for her to stop.

The sun rose earlier in this part of the country than what Scott was used to. He opened his eyes. Diana slept next to him, her breathing even and rhythmic. While he'd spent many summers here with his parents and sometimes only with his father, the place took on a different life with Diana next to him. Love swept up inside him and nearly choked him. How had he ever come to this place in life without her? And to think their separate paths only crossed due to the Match For Love program that both had to be talked into using. Thankfully, the universe was on their side.

"How long have you been watching me?" Diana asked.

Scott looked down bringing her into focus. "Since the beginning of time," he whispered.

Diana smiled and raised her arm to encircle him. They were in his bed, the maroon one. After spending so much time downstairs, they finally made to the bed where a repeat of their lovemaking took most of the night.

"Are you hungry?" he asked.

"Yes." She dragged the word out, letting him know her hunger wasn't for any of the stores in the downstairs kitchen.

Immediately his body started to harden. Scott couldn't believe he could want her again so soon, but he knew he did.

Diana pulled herself up. The sheet and comforter fell from her body revealing her breasts. They were nearly his undoing. His hand caressed the perfect mounds before he knew they had moved. Her eyes closed as his thumbs brushed across the sensitive buds. Diana climbed on top of him and took control of their kiss. Her mouth was like a sweet candy to him. He wanted more and more of it, knowing this was a sweetness without end. It wouldn't give him a stomachache, tooth decay or added weight. It could only make him feel good, make him know the passion and rapture of two people who among the billions on the planet had found each other.

In moments they were joined to each other in the most

intimate way. Their lovemaking was slower than it had been last night. Mornings seemed to warrant that. Scott wanted it to go on for decades, until a wave of emotion gripped him and the pleasure he felt walled up like a huge typhoon and crashed into him. Without realizing it, his head was banging the headboard as the power unleashed by the two of them writhing together took them on a journey of pleasure that was unbridled.

Scott was out of breath and he'd never lost so much control. He would happily have gone on banging his head if Diana continued her drive to pleasure as she had just done. He had never experienced a woman as he had with Diana.

"We're going to have to get out of here," Scott said, each word took a full breath.

"Why?" Diana asked.

"Because if we don't, you're going to kill me, and then you'll have to call the forest service because you can't fly the plane."

"Who says I can't fly the plane?"

A hundred yards from the house in any direction, the forest grew thick and dark. Scott had given her a heavy jacket to wear. Diana didn't think she would need it until the sun barely made it through the tall trees. The temperature was at least twenty degrees lower inside there. Scott held her hand and led her down a path that had once been there, but now the forest had reclaimed it.

She wore boots that belonged to Scott's mother and were a size too large, forcing her to grip the toes. This made walking hard and tiring.

"How far in do we have to go?" She had no idea where they were going.

"Not much farther," Scott answered.

"That could mean anything from a few yards to several miles." She pushed a branch aside. Most of the trees were evergreens. Their bristle needles scratched at her. Frequently she had to dodge one from hitting her in the face. Grabbing at them with her hands left her with red marks against her skin.

Finally, they emerged into a clearing. A few yards ahead of them was a small stream.

"It's beautiful," Diana said. It was like coming upon an undiscovered oasis. The place was surrounded by trees and mountains. Yet this plaza looked almost landscaped.

"This is where my dad and I used to come and talk."

The sun was warm here and Diana grew hot wearing the coat. Undoing the buttons, she heaved herself atop a boulder, bringing her knees up and clamping her hands around them. "Tell me about your dad," she said. "You know I know very little about you. Only that your family is wealthy, you come from Minnesota and you have a house in Maine." She looked back at the path they had come from.

"His name is Kevin and he owns a manufacturing business. They make medical instruments."

Instantly Diana had a picture of heart valves and leg braces in her mind. "He started it making tiny instruments for children's surgery," Scott continued. "From there he went into innovative instruments that kept up with medical technology."

"I apologize," Diana said.

Scott turned to stare at her. "For what?" he asked.

"Your roots are humanitarian, not commercial."

"Maybe not totally commercial," Scott said. "We make a lot of money selling those instruments."

"But they help diagnose and cure illnesses, mainly in children."

He nodded. Diana knew that made him a millionaire

many times over, but he was providing a valuable resource that was needed to save lives. And Scott had followed in his footsteps even if it appeared tangential.

"Is he still running the company?"

Scott nodded. "They'll have to wheel him out of there."

"Are you planning to join him, become the president of the company?"

Scott shook his head. "I'm not interested in that. He's grooming one of my cousins for that position."

"Are you satisfied being a corporate pilot and dropping everything to fly human organs from place to place?"

"I like the freedom, but the life of a pilot is short."

Diana waited for further explanation.

"It's not something you can do into your sixties and retire from. The plane is an unforgiving mistress. She'll test you at every turn. You have to be on the mark every minute, without fail. Or you will fail."

"What does that mean?"

"It means I'll need to prepare to do something else when flying becomes a younger man's job."

"You say that as if you're an old man."

He laughed. "I know I'm not old, but I also know that I need to plan for my future."

"Got something in mind?"

"I have some investments. And I'm a major stockholder in my father's company. I'm sure I'll find something to do." He smiled and came to stand in front of her.

"What about your mom?" Diana asked. She didn't want to be distracted by his closeness, but that was a losing gamble. Whether he was across the room or across the country, he distracted her. "Does she work outside the home or is she running the society of Minneapolis?"

"She'd hate to hear you say that. My mom designs jewelry."

Diana frowned. In the back of her mind, she tried to re-member something. "Thomas. Amera Thomas?"

"Yes," Scott said

"Amera Thomas is your mother?" Incredulity was evi-dent in Diana's voice.

Scott opened his jacket and looked inside. "I'll check my birth certificate, but I'm pretty sure it has her name on it."

"Designs of Amera jewelry appear in all the bridal mag-azines. Her creations sell for tens of thousands of dollars. They are as prominent on the red carpet as any Versace, Armani or Vera Wang gown. I am so impressed."

"I'll tell her you said that." He plucked a pinecone from the ground and pulled out extraneous pieces, then pre-sented it to her. "Now it's your turn."

"My family isn't nearly as interesting. And you already know where I grew up," Diana told him.

"But I don't know who your parents are."

Diana sighed. "My mother is an academic book editor. And my father teaches college mathematics."

"I'm sure there's more to them than that."

"My mother specializes in early European history, but she has worked on books from China, Australia, India and Africa. She's a wonderful woman who finds books change the world and she instilled reading in her children. I can probably recite you part of the text of every book I ever read and every one she ever read to me."

"That's impressive. What about your dad?"

Diana smiled thinking about her dad. "He's the typi-cal absentminded professor. If it weren't for my mother, I don't think he'd be able to find his shoes. Although he's a snappy dresser, my mom picks his clothes out. He'll get on a math problem and forget everything else." She stopped to smile again. "We were a noisy bunch of kids. When I come home sometimes I miss that noise. And when I go to check on my parents' house, I remember the antics we did in some of those rooms."

"Sounds like you had a wonderful childhood."

"I did. We didn't have all the opportunities of the world, but in terms of love and laughter, we had the most."

Without them discussing it, Diana slid down from the rock and into Scott's arms. He hugged her close. "I'm glad," he whispered.

"For what?" Diana asked.

"For being normal."

"I didn't say we were normal." She laughed.

"In my field, I see the terrible things that can happen to children. Knowing that those close to me are *normal* is an exception."

Diana understood that Scott wasn't the rich boy she'd imagined. Something he'd seen or been part of had cut deeply into his emotions and he'd pushed it way down. It defined his character, and she was proud of that character.

Chapter 13

Princeton was another planet to Diana Monday morning. Maine was beautiful. Her time there with Scott had been magical. The stream, the trees, the mountains, the house, and most of all Scott. She felt as if their whole world was contained in that small space stripped out of the forest. They talked to each other the way lovers did, the way people in love did. And they were in love. She loved him more than she ever thought she could love anyone.

"How was it?" Teddy asked the moment Diana walked into the office. She looked as if she wanted to tap each foot in a gleeful dance.

Diana went to her and closed the door. "It was wonderful." Diana spun around the room like a sixteen-year-old who'd been asked to the big dance by the cutest boy in school. That was exactly how it felt. She was Brainiac, Diana 4.0, the girl hiding behind the long hair and the best-looking man on campus had just asked her to the homecoming dance.

"I want you to tell me all about it, but right now, I have to go put down a crisis."

Diana didn't ask Teddy what the emergency was. Teddy could handle it. Diana wanted to think about herself for a moment. She'd done things for others so long she'd forgotten herself. Now she thought of Scott. The two parted only a few hours ago, yet she missed him. She wanted him now…here…today.

But he was unavailable. He had to fly to South Carolina, then to Boston. One of the corporate executives of the biomedics firm had to get there, and Scott was the pilot who took him. Even so, she wanted to return to the house in Maine, with its satellite phone and isolation.

And she wanted Scott to be with her.

Boston was a maze to Scott. With its cobblestone streets next to major highways and historic districts around every corner, he couldn't see how horse and carriage could find the right house, let alone a rented car. Piper and Josh lived in one of those historic areas. Their house was a redbrick attached row house with flower boxes at the windows and a black iron gate that protected three steps up to the front door. In reality it was no different from any other house on the street except for the brass numbers above the black lacquered front door.

Scott opened the gate and ran up the three steps. He punched the doorbell and waited. Inside he heard the scurry of feet as someone approached the door. Piper looked out from one of the side windows. A smile split her face. Scott found himself smiling, too. Even before she opened the door.

"Well, this is a surprise. What are you doing here?"

He came inside and hugged her. "I had a delivery for Mass General. Thought I'd use it as an excuse to get a home-cooked meal."

"Well, you're right on time. I'm just finishing dinner." She started for the kitchen. Scott dropped his hat and coat on the radiator cover near the door and followed her.

"Where's Josh?" he asked, noticing the absence of his brother-in-law.

"He'll be here in a moment. I sent him to get some bread."

"It smells great in here. What are we having?" Scott glanced at the stove.

"Liver and onions."

"Liver?" he frowned. "When did you start eating liver? If I remember correctly your usual description to the word *liver* is—'ugh.' Must be the hormone thing."

"It's weird, but we don't want to talk about eating habits."

"Don't we?" Scott said. "It's not like I get liver and onions every day."

"You didn't come all the way here for liver and onions. By the way, we also have vegetable soup. And yes, I know this is July."

"So what do we want to talk about?"

"We want to talk about *her*—Diana." She passed some plates and silverware. "Set the table."

Scott took them, glad of something to do. The minute she mentioned Diana he felt himself tense. Piper was on the money. She usually was.

"I liked her. She's smart, funny, can talk about just about anything. I hate it when a person can only talk about themselves and whatever their business is. She knows a lot. Did you know she speaks several languages?"

"Yes, I did." The incident at the church came to mind. Scott forced himself not to relive it.

"Some of the wedding stories she told were hilarious." Piper stopped a moment to laugh. She had to be remembering something Diana had relayed.

Scott walked to the cabinet and retrieved glasses. He set them on the table.

"How do you feel about her?" Piper asked.

He stopped and faced his sister. She'd stopped her activities and was looking at him.

"Oh, my God," she said, her voice low as it dawned on her. "You're in love with her."

Scott took a long moment before responding. Then he nodded once. But once was enough for Piper. She sailed across the room and hugged him. "Have you told her?"

"Not yet."

"I'm thrilled," Piper said. Her smile could rival the Charles River.

"About what?"

Both of them turned as someone spoke from the doorway. Josh stood there holding a long bag with a tube of French bread poking out of it.

"Hi, Scott." He came forward and the men shook hands and gave each other a back-clapping hug. "What brings you to Beantown?" Josh went to Piper and kissed her on the mouth.

"My I-didn't-know-my-sister-was-pregnant discovery. Congratulations, by the way."

"Thanks. Did she tell you about the house?"

Scott glanced at his sister.

"Scott's been a little distracted lately. I haven't gotten around to the house. We can talk about it as we eat. Sit down."

Piper cut the bread and added it to the table with some lemon butter.

"You sit down," Jose told her. "I'll serve."

Piper and Scott took seats and Jose filled their plates. "I hope you like liver," he said, lifting an eyebrow. "I've eaten some strange foods since Piper got pregnant."

"French bread with liver and onions isn't that strange?" Piper defended.

"It is if you don't like liver." They laughed.

"So, Scott, when are you buying the ring?" Josh asked. Scott nearly choked.

"Does that mean you haven't bought it yet?" Josh didn't wait for an answer. "Take my advice. When you go to pick it out, take her with you. She'll need to choose her own stone and setting."

He looked at his sister. She nodded and put her own hand up. Her ring had a setting around it that had been added after.

"Even if it is an Amera design, let her choose it."

"So," Piper began. "When are you going to ask her?" Her smile, one of those that said she was ready to join in the planning. Scott could almost see her rubbing her hands together, eager to start. He wondered what she and Diana had really talked about that night at dinner. All Diana had said was a solitary *you*. And then he couldn't get another word out of her.

"Do you think she'll wait until after the baby, so I won't have to wear a maternity dress?"

"I think we should hold off on any plans until the lady accepts."

By Wednesday the construction was driving Diana crazy. There was so much building material and piles of debris she could hardly reach her office. She had to park a few hundred feet way from the building in order to get in. Obstacles were everywhere. Diana held the two cups of coffee she and Teddy shared every day before work began.

"This noise and all these construction materials are hardly conducive to our business." Teddy arrived about the same time. They met in the parking lot.

"It hard to get around them," Diana shouted to Teddy. "And they've practically blocked our entrance. I checked with the fire department, and so far they have not violated any code. But we're not letting him push us away. We leased this place at their insistence, and we're not giving it up."

"I know it's in a convenient location, our lease still has three years to run, we took this property before they built the hospital down the street, and all the trendy establishments weren't springing up, but will our clients cross all this debris to get to our offices?"

"Do you want to move?"

"No, this area is much more convenient for me, too. It's close to both our homes, the area is upscale, and I believe the owners want to rake in more money by throwing us out and charging the next tenant more rent."

Diana nodded. "Also, most of the other services we work with are close by. Moving would cause them an unnecessary inconvenience."

Both women stood looking at the mess the workmen had created.

"Let's see what we can get done before the jackhammers start," Diana said.

She turned, taking the coffee cup she'd set on a pallet of lumber. Teddy screamed. Diana turned back. Teddy was now on the ground.

"Are you all right?"

Teddy didn't answer.

Then Diana saw the blood. Looking back she shouted to the men on the other side of the yard, "Help!" Teddy's leg was bleeding badly. Bending down she pulled some tissues from her purse, along with her cell phone, and began dabbing at the blood. Teddy groaned in pain.

"Hold on, Teddy," Diana soothed. Then she saw the gash on Teddy's leg and knew she needed stitches. "Help!" she shouted again. Teddy had fallen into the pile of lumber and ripped her leg on an exposed nail.

Several men came running. "We need to get her to the hospital," Diana said.

One of them came forward carrying a first-aid kit. He looked at her leg and grabbed something from the kit, which he tied around her leg. Without wasting words, he scooped Teddy into his arms as if she weighed nothing. Teddy cried in pain and turned squeezing the man holding her. Her teeth were clamped on her bottom lip. Diana saw the tears in her eyes and felt her own blur.

"Bring a truck," the one carrying her shouted.

It appeared almost immediately and several of them climbed inside. Teddy whimpered at each bump in the road. With the construction creating an obstacle course, the bumps were plenty. The new hospital was less than a mile from their complex. The staff went into action when they saw Teddy and all the blood. Diana and the men were pushed into a waiting room. After Diana provided all the pertinent information and insurance cards, she returned to the waiting room.

"You're still here?" The three men who'd driven them over stood up.

"How is she?" one of them asked.

"I don't know. I was giving her health information. I want to thank you all." She looked from one to the other. "I couldn't have handled her alone."

"We try not to have accidents, but sometimes they are unavoidable."

"I'm sorry, miss. I put that lumber there. I didn't think…"

"It's all right," Diana said, touching his arm for assurance

"We'll move it right away," the one who'd carried Teddy

said. "We best be getting back now. We have a schedule to meet."

"Thank you," Diana said. "I'll let you know how she is as soon as I find out."

He nodded. The three of them headed toward the door.

What are your names?" Diana stopped them. They all turned back to her. "I'm sure Teddy is going to want to know."

"I'm James, miss." James was a massive guy. He was the one who'd carried Teddy. "I'm the foreman. This is Eddie Layton and Kyle Murray." Eddie had driven the truck and Kyle had administered first aid.

"Thank you again."

James, understanding that she was distraught over her friend, touched her on the shoulder. "She'll be all right," he told her.

The other two nodded. "You call us and we'll come take you home." This again from James. He handed her a dirty slip of paper with the construction company logo on it and a phone number. "It's my cell."

"I will."

"Which one?" Scott shouted. He grabbed one of the workers and hauled him close. He probably scared the man, but Scott was past caring. It could have been Diana. "Which one?" he growled at the man. Scott's heart pounded as if someone was beating it with a mallet. Pain like he'd never felt before seized his chest. The men had just told him that one of the women from the wedding company had been hurt.

"I don't know. James and Eddie took her," the man said.

"Took her where?" Scott tried to lower his voice, but he was beyond control.

"The hospital."

He dropped his hold on the man and was back in his car in a flash. With the precision the car was built to perform with, he sprayed gravel and dust behind him as he took off like a horse out of the starting gate. This was his fault. He'd badgered them to move. When Diana dug her heels in, he drew up a different plan, but it used part of the area her offices occupied. They were there every day, going in and out, negotiating the construction materials. It was bound to cause an accident, and now it had.

Scott must have looked like a madman when he burst through the doors of the emergency entrance. Wildly he looked from one place to another, hoping to find Diana. If she had been hurt he couldn't forgive himself.

"Scott."

He whirled around at the sound of his name. Diana was coming toward him. Relief flooded through him like the Niagara River cascading over the falls. He took off at a dead run. He grabbed her, pulled her into his arms and locked his mouth on hers. His arms traveled all over her as he kissed her. It took a moment before he realized she was not responding. He stopped. Lifting his head, he looked at her.

Diana pushed herself back, and he got his first good look at her. If she wasn't hurt, it had to be Teddy. "How is she?" he asked.

"She cut an artery. If we'd been any farther from this hospital, she'd have bled out."

"I'm sorry." He took a step forward. She moved back.

"Go away. I never want to see you again."

"Diana, I didn't mean for this to happen."

"I truly believe that," she said. "But if you hadn't been so hell-fired to get us out of there, your construction people wouldn't have all that dangerous equipment putting us in harm's way." She took a breath. Scott could see she was trying to keep control of herself. "Teddy almost died." She spoke through clenched teeth, but her voice still broke. "And over what? A little bit of land. Well, we'll move, Scott. Our five-year lease is up in three years. At that time, and not a minute before, you can have the office."

"Diana, I—"

"I'm done talking to you. All further dealings between us can be conducted by our lawyers."

Diana turned and walked away. She held her head up and she didn't hurry her steps, but every line of her body was stiff and unapproachable. Scott wanted to kick himself. He didn't dictate the construction plans, but he'd noticed the hazards of the narrow path they had to get to the office doors.

Scott didn't believe the way his heart ached. He'd never felt this bad before. He'd lost her. He could tell by the way she'd felt in his arms. What was he going to do now?

For the past five years Diana had risen each morning with a smile on her face. Going to work made her happy. Even the pitfalls of difficult mothers and bridesmaids hadn't made her want to pull the covers over her head and hide from the world. But for the past week she'd gone through the motions. It was hard to accept the tone of voice of some of the customers, but so far Diana had managed to keep everything going. Teddy was out of the hospital and forbidden to come into the office.

Diana was working with Teddy's assistant, Renee, to make sure everything went well. Renee was a godsend, and Diana considered herself lucky to have her. She filled in the details and kept everything going in the right direction.

As Diana passed the coffee shop, she remembered when she'd seen Scott and Linda sitting inside by the window. They had cuddled so close, they should have gotten a room instead of making a display for the entire township to see. Diana had stopped going to Edward's after that. Now she made coffee in the office or picked up a cup from the construction lunch wagon that came around for breakfast and lunch. It wasn't Edward's fine blend, but it opened her eyes.

"Damn," she cursed and pulled the car into a parking space. She wasn't going to let Scott or Linda alter her routine. She liked Edward's coffee and she'd go to his shop whenever she wanted. She did not have to talk to Scott just because she bought coffee there.

Diana was lucky. Scott was not in the shop. She ordered for herself and Teddy and continued on to the office. She was back in the car before she remembered Teddy was not in the office. Glancing at the two cups sitting on the middle console, she raised a shoulder and decided she could drink them both. Today was a double-cup day, anyway.

Unsure if she was disappointed or elated at not finding Scott waiting for her, she vowed to make this day different. He was out of her life. She was going to be the person she had been before she filled out that stupid profile and got involved with him. She, Diana Greer, was a businesswoman. She had clients to see and weddings to plan. There had been no time in her life for dating to begin with. Her situation now only confirmed what she already knew— that men were a complication. And that Scott Thomas was someone she could not count on.

He'd changed from the boyish college prankster. Now he was a ruthless businessman and he wanted her out of the office. Diana was going to move. She'd resolved last night to talk to Teddy. They couldn't hold meetings or ask clients to risk hurting themselves to get through the construction. They also had other employees, other consultants that couldn't be put at risk. If they had to, they could take office space on Nassau Street. They could afford it.

But they wouldn't totally relinquish possession of the offices until her contract ended. She could still work from these offices. If she had to meet a potential franchise client, she'd arrange for the face-to-face in the new place.

Arriving at the parking lot, Diana found a clear path to the office doors, although she still had to park in the outer fringes of the lot. She gathered her briefcase and the coffee and closed the door.

"Let me help you," James said. He was a couple of steps away from her when she stood up. Diana wondered if Scott had left instructions that anyone going in and out of the building have safe passage to the door. Of course, he was liable for any accidents that were directly due to the construction. Like Teddy's.

"I'm all right, James," she told him.

Still, he took her briefcase and escorted her to the door. Diana wondered: If he hadn't been so dusty, would he have picked her up and carried her to the door? But then that could open up a whole new set of liability issues.

Inside, the assistants had things under control. Diana went to work on finding a new place to relocate. She called a real estate broker she knew in Princeton and made arrangements to see several places with space to rent. It was while she was talking to him that she thought it would make sense to separate the two offices, although she would have liked them to be fairly close to each other. And having a parking lot brought in more revenue than not having one. But she would miss being with Teddy if the two were separated. Walking into her office and having her come in and relax at the end of the day had become a routine that Diana didn't want to give up.

Mentally shaking herself, she decided to think about that later. When Scott finished all this construction, maybe the place would be better for her and her offices. And maybe he'd be willing to work on a second lease. She was three years from the current lease expiring. By then the construction would be complete.

"Excuse me, Diana."

Diana looked up from her desk several hours later. She'd been engrossed in a new campaign for the franchises. Renee stood in the doorway.

"I'm leaving now. The Garmin wedding is tonight and I need to be at the church early."

"No problem. I'll be there to help you out if you need anything, even if it's just a second pair of hands."

Renee smiled, but she didn't immediately turn to go.

"Is there something else?"

"Well…" There was hesitation in her voice. "I'm not supposed to tell you, but if I don't and anything happens…" She trailed off.

"Teddy has asked you to come and get her or something like that."

Renee's eyes opened wide. "How did you know?"

"Teddy and I have been partners a long time. Friends longer than that." She smiled and relaxed. Renee relaxed, too. "You go on to the church. I'll pick up Teddy. And I'll bring her."

Teddy couldn't have been more surprised when Diana's van arrived instead of Renee. She wore a floor-length gown in a deep wine color. It complemented the reddish highlights in her hair.

"I knew she couldn't keep this quiet," Teddy said as she admitted Diana into her living room.

"Renee was protecting you," Diana told her.

"I'm fine."

"I know you are. That's why I brought a wheelchair and you're going to sit in it."

Teddy decided not to argue. Both of them knew that

argument would get Teddy nowhere. If she wanted to go to this wedding, she'd have to play by Diana's rules. For a moment, Diana wished others would play by her rules.

"Heard from Scott?" Teddy asked, her voice tentative.

"He's no longer a factor in my life. I hate that I ever filled out that profile."

"Tell me the truth. Are you really sorry? Would you feel better if you'd never had any time with him?"

Diana didn't immediately answer. Her heart hurt. She was miserable all the time, and putting on a front that things were normal, that *she* was normal, gave her a perpetual headache. She'd fallen in love with Scott, and there was nothing she could do about it. She'd loved being in his arms. And their lovemaking had been something she wasn't sorry about. He'd made her feel more wonderful, more loved, than anyone ever had.

"Am I sorry?" She hadn't realized she spoken aloud until Teddy said something.

"At least you know now. You don't have to wonder your whole life."

"I know, but that's not a yes or no question."

Diana sat down on the sofa and looked about Teddy's living room.

"What did you like about him?"

Diana smiled. A blanket of warmth settled over her. "I liked the way I felt when he touched me. He'd whisper in my ear or just sit with his arm touching mine."

"And in bed?" Teddy prompted.

Diana's head whipped around, and she looked at her friend. She was about to push the question aside, then decided the truth was better. "Fantastic," she said.

Teddy smiled. "You should talk to him about it."

"The accident brought it all into focus for me. He still

wants us out of the offices and he's doing everything to make that happen. Even making love to me."

Teddy didn't say anything. Diana knew neither of them could definitively say that Scott's actions hadn't been to achieve the goal of getting them to move.

"Well, he's won," Diana said.

"What do you mean?"

She looked at Teddy. "I think we should move. I talked to an agent this morning and I have several places to look at in the next few days."

"I thought we were going to tough it out."

"That was before you got hurt," she told Teddy. "I'm not giving up the offices." Diana went on to explain her plan. "We can't risk having one of our clients hurt, and we certainly can't let it be one of us or the other consultants. Our only option is to move to better surroundings."

"And then what?"

"I don't know. I was thinking of separating the sales offices from the consulting side."

"I would hate that," Teddy said.

"Me, too," Diana admitted. "We can talk about it later."

"Yeah," Teddy said. "Right now, let's go to a wedding."

Chapter 14

Scott was camped on her doorstep when Diana got home from the wedding. She'd stayed longer than usual, telling herself she was enjoying it. But she really didn't want to face an empty house. And then she'd had to take Teddy home. By the time she'd turned into her driveway it was two o'clock in the morning. Scott's car was parked to one side of her two-car garage. She saw him as the van's lights flashed over the porch.

Groaning, she thought, *Not now.* She was not in the mood for a confrontation. She wondered how long he'd been there. Pressing the button to raise the garage door, she drove inside and closed the van's door. Scott opened the door for her the moment she unlocked it.

"I want to talk to you," he said.

"Well, I don't want to talk to you. Now would you leave my garage?"

"Not until I've said what I came to say. You've been avoiding me, not answering or returning my calls. My only alternative was to come here and wait."

"Sorry to inconvenience you."

"Don't be sarcastic. It doesn't fit you."

"Why not?" she countered. "Because the Diana you

remember would just keep walking and never reply to the barbs you direct at me? Well, that Diana died. Now you have me to deal with."

Diana was going to have to talk to him sometime. They lived in the same city, so they would inevitably run into each other. She knew she might as well get this over with.

Leaving everything in the van, she got out and went into the house. Her head hurt from all the loud music and dancing she'd done. She hadn't had much to drink, but she'd had a couple of glasses of champagne. The garage door led into the mudroom, which led in turn to the kitchen. A light over the sink provided a small amount of illumination. She hit the switch that threw the kitchen into bright light. The sudden change hurt her eyes. Diana was sure stress had something to do with it, and with Scott on her heels, it was bound to get worse before it got better.

"Would you like something to drink?" she offered, her manners holding from the amount of customer service training she'd had.

"No," he said.

She opened the refrigerator and took out a bottle of water. She opened a nearby cabinet and grabbed a bottle of aspirin. Scott's larger hand took it away from her.

"Hey," she said.

"If this is because you have a headache, fine. If it's because of stress or drinking, they won't help."

Diana twisted the cap on the water bottle and took a long drink. Then she walked into the living room where another low-wattage light burned. She flopped down on the sofa.

Scott came in and took the chair across from her, the same one he'd sat in when she'd woken up with her hangover a couple of weeks ago. It felt like a lifetime ago.

Diana kicked her shoes off and her hair had begun to

fall. Reaching up she pulled the pins holding it free. The masses tumbled about her shoulders. She stifled a yawn.

"All right, what do you want to say?"

"I'm in love with you."

Scott didn't know what reaction he would get, but having Diana stare at him as if she'd turned to stone was not one of them.

"Say something," he commanded.

"What would you like me to say?"

"'I love you' would be nice."

"It would," she agreed, but did not return the phrase.

This was going all wrong. Scott had imagined the conversation while he waited on the porch for her to return, but this was not meeting his expectations. He wanted to leave and stood up. Obviously, Diana was in no mood to listen to him or to even consider his declaration. He wouldn't continue to wear his heart out where she could see it and do nothing about it.

"I thought you felt the same way about me," he said. "But I can see I was wrong."

Scott didn't wait for her to say more. He took one last chance to reach her. He hauled her up from the sofa and into his arms. Squeezing her hard enough to stop her breathing, he found her mouth and captured it in a long, soul-searching kiss.

Diana didn't react in his arms. She didn't resist him, but she didn't participate, either. After a moment he released her and stepped back. Without a word, he left her, closing the door with a soft click. Yet he heard the echo of lost love reverberating behind him.

"You weren't wrong," Diana said very slowly after he was gone. "I love you. I've been in love with you since I fell into your arms that first day I walked onto campus." But there was no one there to hear her.

Teddy returned to full-time work, and Diana had to admit she was glad to have the help. Handling the business totally alone was something she didn't want to do again. The two could be away for vacations or the occasional emergency, but weeks of recovery had laid a heavy burden on her. Diana thought it was time to train some of the assistants to take over when needed.

"You'll never guess who called," Teddy said, coming into Diana's office.

It was late in the day. Time for the two of them to sit and talk for a few minutes before leaving for the night.

Diana turned around to see the Cheshire cat grin on her friend's face. "You're kidding."

Teddy head slowly moved side to side. Diana started to laugh. "How many is this? Three? Four?"

"We are about to meet husband number four."

"Who's the mark this time?" Diana asked.

"Husband-to-be is Giles Marchand," Teddy said.

"Sounds English." Diana's eyebrows rose.

"He is, and he owns a chain of department stores."

"Leave it to Jessica Halston-Wills-Commings-Olmstead to find an English lord as her next husband," Diana said, using the last names of Jessica's former husbands.

"I didn't know he was a lord." Teddy took a seat in front of Diana's desk.

"Knowing Jessica, I'm surprised he isn't a king." Diana glanced at the bridal veil lying across the conference table in the corner of her office. "I suppose we're to do our usual extravagant affair," Diana said.

Teddy nodded.

"If she keeps this up, we can count on her to carry payroll and keep us afloat every two or three years."

"This time she wants an English Court wedding," Teddy said. "She's coming in tomorrow to begin the planning process."

"Are we going to England and using Westminster Abbey and all the ensuing grounds?" Diana teased.

Teddy screwed up her face. "Only a little short of that. She wants it at Saint Patrick's Cathedral."

Diana's head came up quickly. "She's not Catholic."

"Tell her that."

Getting out of the SUV, Diana felt a little nonplussed. James didn't immediately come to help her to the door. None of the other workmen came over, either. In fact, the site had only a few men working. She wondered what was going on. Collecting the things she needed to carry in, Diana could have used help today. She was loaded down with books, cases, samples, her briefcase and purse.

Juggling it all, she used her hip to bump the door shut and click the key fob to lock it. Getting inside the door was another circus-style act. Once inside, she dropped her briefcase next to an open office door. Several people looked up at the noise.

James came out. "Can I help you?" He picked up the briefcase and Diana got a look inside the room.

"What is this?" she said, going inside. She put her huge packages on a chair and walked over to a glass-enclosed case. Inside was a mock-up of the complex. Immediately she recognized the building she worked in. If she had any problem identifying it, all she needed to do was read the label. *Weddings by Diana* was printed in block letters on the small roof of a building in the center of the complex.

"This is the design of the area we're building," James

said. "It's going to be a medical complex for families of children with catastrophic conditions."

Diana's eyes roamed over the small-scale model that took up the entire surface of a conference table.

"Why is there a playground?"

"Some of the families will live here." He pointed to the housing area. There were semidetached houses and town homes. "Probably the families have other children. This is a place for them to play."

Diana went on to look over the mock-up.

"The major changes have to do with the new hospital." He pointed toward the completed building where they had taken Teddy after her accident. "This area is only a mile from the hospital. Families can visit their children and then have a safe place to come to."

James pointed out a day-care center, a nursery school, a health center and fitness facilities, even recreational areas for young adults and parents.

Diana glanced over the entire complex. It was obvious her office building was not originally part of the model.

She now realized Scott had bought this entire area to build up for families in need. Why hadn't he explained that to her? Not that she would have listened or believed him at the time. She thought he was just being the same overgrown kid he was in college, and that he wanted her to move for no good reason. He'd never said he was building a medical facility and that his efforts would help families in need—or that her office stood in the way of his plans.

"This has got to have cost a fortune," Diana said. "These families won't be able to afford to live here for extended periods." This property was in Princeton. Land was extremely expensive.

"There will be no charge," James told her.

Diana looked up at the big man. "No charge? How can that be? Especially if this is a viable business."

"I'm not sure of the full details of how that happens, but Mr. Thomas said it was partly family money and partly a perpetual trust that will keep it going."

Part family money, Diana thought. This meant Scott was backing it himself. A wave of love rushed through her. She'd been so wrong about him. He was trying to make the world a better place, and she looked like the ugly capitalist standing in his way.

Well, she wouldn't any longer. She'd talk to Teddy today, and they would figure out how long it would take for them to set up temporary offices in another place. The papers Scott's lawyer had left with her were still upstairs in her office. She'd sign them and send them to him today. There would be some disruption until they were settled, but she was sure they could handle it if they worked together.

"James, what are they putting in this building?" She pointed at the one with her company name on the roof.

"We're leaving that one alone except for the outside. It'll be redone to look like the others, and there will be a private entrance and private parking lot."

"I see." His words made her feel smaller. "What was the original plan for it?"

"Doctor's and dental offices. But Mr. Thomas changed it before construction began."

"Why?" Diana asked unconsciously. She didn't realize she'd said it out loud. She knew why Scott had done it—to placate her.

"Not sure," James said. "But it's providing jobs in this economy, upgrading the hospital to a first-class level and providing a valuable service to kids and parents in need."

"I didn't know," she whispered, but this time only she could hear it.

Diana gathered her belongings. They felt even heavier than they had when she'd gotten them out of the van. "Thank you," she told James and gave him a smile. He was a nice guy, and she could tell that he believed in what Scott was doing.

She turned back. "James, do you have children?"

He smiled. "Three. They are the light of my life and I'm thankful that all of them are healthy, but at any moment any family could need this facility."

Giving his big arm a squeeze, she said nothing, but let him know she understood.

In her office several minutes later, she located the papers and glanced through them. The offer was very fair. She signed them and walked over to Teddy. After explaining what she'd seen downstairs, Teddy signed them, too.

"Where do we go now?"

"We started this in my great room. We could go back there until we find something more suitable. You and I could share that room, and if we remove the furniture in the dining room and the downstairs office, we can put the other consultants in there."

"What about the real estate agent?"

"He had some promising space. None of it was as ideal as we have here, but we may have to give up some amenities for the sake of moving."

"Diana, this is a good thing. Don't look like you've lost your best friend. We'll survive."

Diana smiled at her, but her attitude didn't change. "I know we will. And we'll be better than before."

"That's the spirit," Teddy said. "Why don't we celebrate? Go somewhere after work and forget the troubles of the day."

"What do we have to celebrate?"

"Good citizenship. We're giving up our space for needy children."

Diana felt a little better after Teddy said that. And even if it was later than it should have been, they were doing something good.

"Are we?" Teddy asked after a moment.

"Are we what?"

"Are you concerned about unknown needy children or are you really interested in the man providing for them?"

Diana wasn't one to lie to herself or her friend. "I'm not sure," she said, truthfully.

"You're having problems resolving what your mind tells you and what your heart wants?"

Diana weighed her words for a moment. "He hurt you, Teddy," Diana stated.

"True. And it was serious, but I'm not holding a grudge."

"You think I should forgive and forget?"

"I think you should follow your heart."

"My heart says run to him, but I'm not sure that's the best course of action."

"You could be hurt."

She nodded.

"Are you afraid to take the chance?" Teddy asked.

Diana looked at her. In no way did she appear to have had an accident that could have claimed her life. And she appeared to be giving Diana permission to return to the man who caused her accident. Inadvertedly caused, she amended.

"Diana," Teddy spot softly. Diana looked at her. "Take the chance."

The phone in Scott's hand nearly fell to the floor. "What?" he said. It was past seven o'clock, but he and his lawyer worked late hours. Both were still in their offices.

Scott had just returned from a flight and was in the process of filing out the necessary FTA paperwork.

"It came by messenger early this afternoon," the lawyer said. "I was in court and only went through the mail a few minutes ago."

"What were her conditions?"

"She made none. The pages are as pristine as they were when we delivered them. She made no changes."

"And both women signed them?"

"Both signatures are on it."

"Did she give a reason?" Scott asked.

"Nothing. The envelope contained only the contract. Nothing else. Not a letter, not even a sticky note."

"I don't understand," Scott said. He was speaking more to himself than to his lawyer on the other end of the phone.

"Don't question it. You have what you wanted. Now you can go ahead with your original plan for the entire complex."

Scott agreed and rang off. He had what he wanted, but what about Diana? Where was she going? She'd held out on moving for so long, and now without a word of explanation the papers arrived. Something must have happened. Was it Teddy's accident? Diana had refused to speak to him since Teddy had been hurt. He wondered where she was. He hadn't seen her in days. She could do her franchise work from her home. If she needed to take a trip, Teddy or a limousine could take her to the airport without Scott knowing about it.

But he wanted to know where she was. He wanted her close enough to touch, to hold, kiss and make violent love to. He wanted to wake up with her and go to sleep each night with her warm body folded into his. He'd never felt this way about anyone. Until the Match For Love service put them together, he'd have said there was no way she was the one. But he was thinking that not only was she the one, she was the *only* one.

Picking up his cell phone, he dialed her number. He didn't expect her to answer. She hadn't answered any of his other calls. And he was rewarded with the same voice mail message. He'd stopped leaving messages days ago. His number would appear as a missed call, and she would know it was him. She would know he wanted to talk to her. He wanted to explain that he couldn't live without her. He wanted to tell her he loved her, but that was something he couldn't do over a phone. It required an in-person declaration.

Scott was sure she loved him, too. No one could act the way she had when they were making love and be faking it. Being with her was like having fun when they were doing nothing. Her smile, the way she laughed and talked to him. All these intangible things told him that the two of them were in love. But Diana was putting up barriers. He didn't know why. At least not totally. Some of it had to do with his friends and the way not only they, but he also had treated her. And continued to treat her.

Had she had enough? Was she no longer up for the fight with him. Even a fight that put the two of them in the same room. And if he could get her in the room, he could explain.

Scott grabbed his suit jacket and left the office. If she wouldn't answer his call, he'd go to her house. She had to come home sooner or later. And he'd be there waiting for her when that Porsche turned into the driveway.

Five hours later Scott stood up yawning. Raising his arms over his head, he stretched, working the kinks out of muscles that had been stationary too long. Obviously, Diana was better at holding out than he was. It was after one in the morning and there was no sign of her. Giving up, he headed back toward the center of town.

His fingers grasped the steering wheel tight enough to break it. The woman was driving him crazy, the same way she'd done all those years ago when they were in school together. She hadn't known it then. Now he wasn't so sure.

Chapter 15

Scott looked up at the black-and-white building on Nassau Street. It looked like something one would find in a Swiss village instead of a college town by the Raritan Canal. It had taken him two days to find where Diana had moved her offices. He wouldn't have thought anyone could relocate that fast. And indeed she hadn't. Everything from the walls down was gone from the offices he had asked her to move out of. The desks and credenzas, kitchen equipment, everything that was too heavy for her and her staff to carry remained, but the files, samples, photographs, books and everything that decorated the place and made it a working office was gone.

Scott was unused to Diana giving up. It wasn't like her, wasn't in her nature. But he had the contract she'd signed. And like his lawyer had said, there wasn't a mark on it except for her and Teddy's signatures. They had vacated the premises without a word. Scott asked James if anyone had helped them move. James's answer was negative. No one had even seen them move out. In fact, James was unaware they were gone.

But this was their new location. Scott checked the area. It was the busiest part of the township. While that would be good at times and for some types of businesses, it wasn't for weddings. Diana didn't work on volume, nor did she rely on walk-ins. So why would she accept space here?

Scott went into the building and checked the directory. Weddings by Diana was on the top floor. Taking the elevator, he rode the slow mechanism to the top and got off. The corridor was well lit, and led to legal offices and dental facilities. The Weddings by Diana logo was on the door at the end of the hall. Scott knocked softly and opened the door. He didn't know what to expect. She'd commanded a lot of space in his facility. Here the space was cramped with boxes and books stacked in disorder.

He heard Teddy speaking in a back room. The other consultants seemed to be in each other's way. He didn't see Diana as he looked around. Finally, Teddy came out of the back room and stopped when she saw him. She no longer sat in the wheelchair, but she was clinging to the wall. She had obviously left her crutches behind when she came to the door.

"Scott," she said, her voice low with surprise.

"Where's Diana?" he asked.

"Out of town."

He wasn't sure that was true, but he didn't press the point. "What are you doing here?"

"Unpacking." Her clipped one-word answer stung him.

"Why did you leave?"

"Wasn't that what you wanted? To get your space back so you could complete your facility? Well, you have it."

"Where's Diana?"

"She doesn't want to talk to you," Teddy said.

"So is she really out of town?"

"Yes." Teddy's chin rose half an inch, challenging him for questioning her veracity.

Scott looked around. There were a couple of doors in

the office. Both were open and he could see inside them. Diana was not there.

"Would you like to leave a message?" The question was delivered as if he was a tradesman who'd come in with a package that needed a signature.

"I'd like to talk to her."

"Good luck with that," Teddy said and turned back to the room where she'd entered.

He looked at the other women in the room. Two of them only stared back at him. The third one shook her head as if to say she knew nothing.

Scott turned and left the office. He returned to the elevator, pushed the call button and waited. The door opened. At the same time, Scott stepped toward the small space and Diana stepped out of it. They walked into each other.

"Diana!"

"Scott!"

They both spoke at the same time.

"Why did you leave without a word?" he asked.

Diana stepped back as if she needed space. Behind her was the elevator and Scott followed her inside. The door closed and he hit the stop button. He was going to talk to her and if it had to be here, then so be it.

"Wasn't that what you wanted from Day One?"

"Of course, but I didn't expect you to sneak out in the middle of the night and move into space that is obviously too small for your needs."

"The space is adequate for our needs. Teddy and I will adjust and it won't be long before we're either settled in or finding new space.

Diana stared at Scott.

"Why are you looking like you lost your best friend? I thought you'd be happy that we were gone. You have your space and you can build your dental and doctor's offices.

The wall around the parking lot doesn't need to be there, and there won't be a blight on the layout you've chosen." She paused a moment.

"Scott, you haven't kicked us out. What you're doing, what you're building for the kids and families is more important than a bridal business's needs. We feel good about giving up our space for the purposes you have in mind." She looked at him. "Our brides will understand why we moved, and they'll be fine with it. Most of our business is done outside the office, anyway."

"Are you sure?"

"I'm sure," she said.

"I don't understand you at all," Scott said.

Diana smiled at that.

"That's exactly what I mean," he said.

"I don't understand," she said.

"I say I don't understand you and you're smiling. Why would that make you smile?"

"I've never been called a mystery woman." She cast a trusting eye at him. "I like it."

Scott looked perplexed and Diana understood his confusion. She had been one way and then the other. He probably wondered who she was today. The consistent Diana 4.0. In her wake was a new Diana.

"I have a secret to tell you."

He moved closer to her. Diana felt the familiar fear of anticipation. He didn't know how he would react to her words. She'd reacted badly to the same ones when he'd said them.

"What is it?" Scott asked.

"You told me once that you loved me. I never answered you. I didn't return the sentiment."

Diana felt him grow still.

"Well, I am in love with you. I fell in love with you the first day I saw you on campus. From that day to this one, I've never changed my feelings. I love you."

Scott's arms were around her before she could move. He pulled her close, and she felt as if she could no longer breathe without his support.

She reached up and pulled his mouth to hers. Diana felt the hard thudding of his heart against her ear.

"I love you, too," he said. "I don't think I could go another day with coming back and forcing you to say it."

"No force necessary," she told him. "I love you now. I'll love you forever."

"Will you marry me?" he asked.

Diana felt he was holding his breath. She nodded.

At the end of the aisle on her wedding day, Diana paused and looked at the assembled group. Her father held her arm. When she glanced at him, his eyes were glistening. "Don't you start," she told him. "If you cry, I will, too."

He sniffed and they faced the altar. Scott stood smiling at her. A wave of love washed over her. This was her choice. This was the man she wanted to spend her life with. She wanted to have children and watch them playing with their dad on the front lawn. She wanted to make him happy.

Teddy took her place as maid of honor. Her bridesmaids smiled from their positions arrayed across the front, waiting for her to begin her walk down the aisle. Everything was as perfect as Diana could wish it to be. Her ceremony wasn't the showplace event she and Teddy planned for their clients. This was a small service in the open air, on the campus of Princeton University right at the kissing spot. With a few of their most intimate friends and family. The chairs were all filled. Scott's friends watched.

After today they would no longer be able to call him the last bachelor.

When the "Wedding March" began, everyone stood. Diana took the first step toward a new life.

* * * * *